THE SLAVES OF LOMOORO

by

CHARLES NUETZEL

WRITING AS "ALBERT AUGUSTUS, JR."

The Borgo Press
An Imprint of Wildside Press

MMVII

CONTENTS

This edition is being offered with a bow to the master:

EDGAR RICE BURROUGHS
(1875-1950)

He inspired this writer and countless other Authors to follow his example

We All Salute His Memory!

INTRODUCTION

This is a special book for me, on several different levels. For one, it was my first SF book. And when it was published I used my late brother's name as a byline, instead of my own. The reason for that is, in itself, a simple story.

But to get to the very beginning, before bylines were even a consideration, even before the time when I actually became a writer.

As indicated elsewhere, I have long had an interest in the literary worlds of Edgar Rice Burroughs. That started when I was thirteen or fourteen, if memory serves me right.

My folks lived in West Los Angeles, which is, in effect, something like a small mountain range distant from Tarzana. When we moved in 1948 to Encino (in the San Fernando Valley), just one town slightly "northeast" of Tarzana, I found a local bookstore where I could continue buying Burroughs' books, wholly unaware, at the time, how close I was to the actual living, breathing author himself!

Well, the owners of the store ended up not only telling me about Edgar Rice Burroughs living nearby, but that they could arrange, at no extra cost to me, to have some of my books autographed by the man himself. It isn't hard to guess what happened next.

Sad to say, I never met Burroughs in the flesh. But I still have a couple of the books he signed, right within sight of where I'm sitting right now. I was told later by his secretary that these were the last books he ever signed. And the handwriting is somewhat shaky, to be sure. He was ill in the hospital at the time, and not long thereafter he died at home.

It wasn't until sometime later that I actually discovered Edgar Rice Burroughs, Inc., located in a small, Spanish-style building on the south side of Ventura Boulevard just a few miles away. This is where I found many surprising things, including a long list of unpublished ERB stories. I also, of course, got to see some of the original book cover paintings that were hanging on the walls. The most thrilling event for me was being escorted into the writer's private office, seeing his desk and the wall full of books of the published editions of his works.

I was more than impressed.

During this period of my life I was a young fan and collector of Burroughs' works, which even then were becoming next to impossible to find. This was before the publishing boom of the 1960s, which brought much of the master's novels back into print. I was able easily to locate the Mars novels, the Tarzan books, and very little else. Secondhand bookstores became my usual Saturday hideaways. I eventually tracked down all of ERB's published works, outside of *The Lad and the Lion* and *Back to the Stone Age* (although I had the latter in serial form). Burroughs' secretary eventually found me a copy of *Lad*. She was a lovely person, generous and very friendly to a young fan. I still have pleasant memories of her.

Slaves of Lomooro is my personal tribute to the writer, and while it doesn't approach the master's work, I hope it will satisfy the fan. The original manuscript was too long to fit the size requirements of the publisher, so it was trimmed quickly by a friend; the original version has long been lost, and I resisted any attempt to restore it.

When the book was published in 1969, I wanted to keep it separate from *Swordmen of Vistar* and the two Noomas books, so I used the byline, Albert Augustus, Jr. My father (Albert Augustus Nuetzel, Sr.) had died shortly before this, and so my choice of a pen name constituted both a tribute to him, and to the memory of my infant brother, who had died shortly after birth.

The novel had the following inscription:

6

**"To my mother, Betty, this first science
fiction book is lovingly dedicated."**

When I was very young, I started calling my parents by
their given names, Betty and Al; for some reason, they
thought this was cute, and allowed me to continue doing this.
Some folks were shocked by the casualness of our family,
but to me it was simply a reflection of the deep affection,
love, and closeness which have continued throughout the
years—and still remains with me.

I hope the book finds a new audience in its second print
edition. I've made a few corrections and I've tweaked a few
scenes, but not very many. And I hope a few of my young
fans and readers will take the time to ferret out the works of
Edgar Rice Burroughs (some of which are available from
Wildside Press), and try them for themselves.

—Charles Nuetzel
Thousand Oaks, California
July 2006

THE SLAVES OF LOMOORO, BY CHARLES NUETZEL

CHAPTER ONE

Crash Landing

A raging storm slashed through the jungle world, muffling the crash as the ship plunged through layer upon layer of matted branches and lacy purple foliage. Finally it came to rest some twenty feet from the planet's surface, shuddered, and was still. Its two-month voyage was finally ended.

Inside the craft, two men and a woman lay sprawled among the wreckage in the ship's small control room.

The tallest of the two men was six foot three, massive and muscular; he was dressed in the silver gray uniform of the Galactic Federation Space Service. Captain's bars were laced into the shoulder pads. Black hair, cropped close, framed the handsome, evenly chiseled face. The rise and fall of his chest was the only indication that he still lived.

The storm outside snapped off the tops of trees and whipped them along in the raging wind. Darkness fell over the world; the storm slowly faded away as the total black of night enveloped the jungle. Then darkness too passed, and the large, hot sun moved up from the horizon.

The uniformed man moved slightly and groaned, but his eyes remained shut.

Captain Jon Handon was first aware of physical pain; a pounding at his temples. He forced himself to concentrate.

He was a spaceman in the Intergalactic Federation of Lacus Patrol, on his way to the War Sector after two months on leave. He had been a professional soldier ever since his twenty-first birthday—the legal age for enlisting in the Space Service. For eight years all he had known was war, followed by weeks off at some space port, almost living in the bars and in the company of women.

Since childhood on the planet Valsol, Jon had dreamed of joining the Patrol as his father had done. Mal Handon had become Major-General, then was killed in a battle with one of the Splinter System navies.

Memories of the past crept into his mind like sand trickling through a clogged sieve, but nothing of the immediate past would sift through.

The death of his mother some five years before had left Jon without any family ties. On his last leave he had returned home to look up a girl, a school friend. But she wanted him to settle down, stay at home, be a family man—something quite impossible for Jon Handon, professional soldier spaceman.

Now, lying in the dimensionless darkness of ebbing pain, Jon wondered if he should have stayed on Valsol, settled down, become a desk officer.

Suddenly, as if some dam had burst, the rush of held-back memory all but overwhelmed him. *Naltolis,* the space liner on which he had been returning to the war zone, had, after two weeks of flight, jarred unexpectedly back to normal space, leaving the dimensionless void of hyper-space through which interstellar travel and speeds faster than the speed of light were possible. Somebody had tampered with the hyper-drive unit—probably an agent from the other side. They were to continue on to the nearest civilized planet at normal speed—something under 100,000 miles per hour. But even this hope was shattered when the engineers discovered that the ship's engines had developed a buildup of radioactive feedback and must be immediately abandoned.

Jon had left his cabin and gone directly to the scout-boat assigned to him and nine other passengers. Mari Dorna and Red Fendricks were already there. They were securing themselves in the bucket seats when the voice of the liner's commander came over the scout-boat speaker. "Leave immediately! Leave immediately! All passengers in scout-boats leave immediately!"

10

Jon had piloted almost every kind of ship, and had therefore been put in charge of this scout-boat during their first practice day. He closed the air lock and pulled the takeoff lever. They soared away from the space liner, building up speed.

A couple of minutes later something silent and deadly lit up space from behind them. Jon watched the view screen in horror as the space liner they had so recently left, and all its remaining passengers, simply stopped existing in that flashing explosion.

Jon assumed command of the scout-boat immediately. Red Fendricks accepted this, but the woman objected.

Mari Dorna had objected to Jon from the first night on board the space liner. They had eaten at the same table in the dining hall. Jon had never seen such an attractive face, so lovely a body. The upsweep of her pert nose, the innocence in her soft blue eyes, the full red lips, all combined to hypnotize him from the beginning. But when he invited her to go dancing, Mari had quickly and coldly put him in his place. Her father was the owner of one of the largest industrial complexes in this section of the Federation— Dorna Enterprises—and Jon Handon, spaceman, was hardly fit to mix socially with her. Mari's direct "No!" had all but put it in words. From that moment on their conversation had been coldly formal, yet Jon could hardly keep his eyes off her.

He had mixed feelings about her being with them in the scout-boat. They would have to get along together for some time, and he wondered whether Mari Dorna could get along with anybody outside of her upper-class society crowd.

Surprisingly, after the immediate shock over the space liner's fate had worn off, Mari offered to take over the cooking duties. But she pointed out that she hoped the two men would allow her as much privacy as possible, and respect her rights as a Citizen of the Federation.

For two months they were to live in the cramped quarters. The scout-boat contained two sections—a cabin with five bunks and five cushioned seats, and a small compartment for eating, cooking, and disposal of wastes. Thus half of the possible ten passengers would be able to sleep while the others sat up, awake in the chairs.

The scout-boats were supplied with enough food in table form to last a year, a star chart book of the immediate systems that surrounded the space liner's route, and one space service atomatic handgun, with one hundred atomatic pellets which served both as explosive bullets for the gun and as hand explosives when a cap at the side was punctured by a sharp object—this latter use was handy in emergencies. Since Jon had his own atomatic gun, issued to him in the space service, both men would be armed if or when they landed on a planet.

Jon quickly explained the standard plan of operation to his two companions. They would find an Earth-type planet, land and send an SOS radio signal. In time, help would come—if they were lucky.

Immediately after leaving the mother ship, Jon had taken out the star chart and searched for the nearest Earth-type planet. He discovered a world called G-Y287 that was not too far from their general location in space, and on the same course their liner had been taking before exploding. Clearly, the liner's Captain had been heading for this planet. The chart book gave little information, but enough. It was an obscure planet, far from the normal Federation boundaries of colonized systems. The rating for colonization was Class-A—perfect for human survival. A footnote supplied one hint as to why it had not been settled:

> Though Class-A in atmosphere and livability, its surface is about seven-tenths water. There are two rather large land bodies of about a million square miles each. The rest of the planet is dotted by hundreds of islands ranging from one to a thousand square miles. Ideal for a resort planet. It is a tropical world. But the system to which it belongs has no other solid planets, and it has no moon. It is unprofitable for colonization at this time. Owned by Fed-Co-Interstellar Company.

Jon learned in the index of companies that the owner

was a firm which had been out of business for some five hundred years. G-Y287 was, for all practical purposes, a lost planet.

That was all they knew about the planet until they went into orbit around it a couple of months later. The sight of the purplish world below them, almost completely covered by water, had been breathtaking.

The relationship between the three passengers was now friendly though impersonal. As long as the two men forgot that Mari was a woman, they were able to get along fine.

"Do you think we'll find any of the other passengers from the liner?" Mari asked Jon. "They surely must have headed for this world, too."

"There's a good chance. I only wish the laser receiver worked." He shrugged. "And with these instruments shot..." He indicated the half dozen unmoving dials on the control board.

Even then, the landing should have gone well. All he had to do was pull out of orbit and pick out one of the continents, then the rest was easy. What went wrong was the tornado-like storm.

Sitting in the pilot's bunk, Jon went through the motions which had been automatic with him for years. A spaceman learned early in life how to land almost any kind of small ship.

The large land mass was a hilly continent which rose to a mountainous center. The outer regions were rolling plains and deserts which slowly blended into thick jungle that covered most of the land, then finally disappeared into snow-capped mountains.

Jon tried to land near the coast, along the rolling plains. They entered the atmosphere and dropped to ten thousand feet. Then suddenly a storm hit with such force that their scout-boat was snatched up like a feather.

Both Mari and Jon were ripped from their bunks and thrown about the small cabin as the scout-boat was forced along the current of the storm.

Jon fought his way back to the bunk and tried to get to the controls, but the ship plunged downward, spun, then twisted about like a top gone wild.

13

* * * * * * *

As Jon became aware of his surroundings, his thoughts turned to Mari. Was she alive?

During their time together in the scout-boat, Jon had come to admire Mari's courage. It had been difficult for her, but she had handled herself well. Mari had been on her way home from a university extension course. She was single and planned on remaining so until turning twenty-five. Her family had arranged a marriage with a suitable young man, son of a wealthy exporter on Tarrio. Her family had been too busy to give her much love and attention. Yet, as Mari had explained, most rich children got little chance to really know their parents because of the social activities which took such people across the Galaxy.

Jon squinted painfully at the shattered remains of the scout-boat cabin, hanging about him like distorted images from Hell. A few feet to his right he spotted Mari, lying against one of the bunks. A large rip in her snug slacks revealed a blood-spattered thigh.

Jon moved to her. The cut in her leg appeared to be bloody but minor. He studied her face for some sign of returning consciousness. "Mari! Mari!"

Then Mari's eyes opened, large, blue, bewildered. For a moment she simply stared up at him.

Then: "We crashed..." She frowned and started to move, then froze, seeing the blood-caked rip in her slacks.

"Nothing serious," Jon quickly assured her "Everything else okay?"

She hesitated in thought, then nodded. "God knows how! How about Red?"

Red Fendricks, the third member of their group, was a large barrel-chested man with deep-set, dark, brooding eyes, a square jaw and hawk nose. He came from the planet of Candor and had been raised in the back streets of the capitol, Candor City. His occupation remained a mystery, and he found polite conversation difficult.

Jon quickly turned to Red, who was doubled up against the door to their small kitchen. He carefully raised Red's

14

head and then rested it back against the door.

"I think he's okay," he reported. "We were lucky."

Mari came to her feet and stared at Red. "We were all lucky. Maybe too lucky." Her voice took on a note of hysteria. "Oh, God!" Mari's fists doubled up and pounded her thighs. "Oh, why?"

Jon leaped to his feet and grabbed Mari. "Snap out of it!" He shook her violently.

Mari stared at him, then slowly she began to relax. Hands trembled up to cover her face. "I'm...sorry. It's just that everything piled up.... Well, where to now?"

"Survive. As best we can!" Jon told her.

Laughter suddenly exploded in the cabin.

"You two musta had your skulls cracked!" Red came to his feet like a bull gathering itself for a charge.

"Are you all right?" Jon asked.

"Fine. Better than you two! Rockets, man! Look at this mess!" He waved his large arms in the air.

The ship looked as if some giant hand had ripped it apart. The bunks were partly torn from the walls; the floor was buckled in the middle. Personal property was scattered around the cabin.

Jon shook his head. "Well, don't stand here! Let's gather what we can, take what's good and get the...get out of this ship!"

Mari objected. "We can't go out there!"

Red laughed. "Look, we're here on this space ball and we gotta make the best of it. We can't stay here in the ship for the rest of our lives."

"But that's jungle out there!" Mari cried, pointing.

Jon and Red moved to her side.

The ship was surrounded by a tangle of thick foliage and layers of interwoven branches which held them suspended some twenty feet from the ground.

Jon turned to Mari. "There's simply nothing else to do now."

"But we could use this as a..."

Before she could finish, they were startled by the sound of metal scraping against wood.

"We have to leave, and fast!" Jon motioned the other

two to hurry.

"The food, supplies, the radio!" Red cried.

"Forget it!" Jon ordered. "Just the atomatic gun! We don't have time for anything else."

Another cracking sound burst from outside and Jon hurriedly stepped out onto the bullet nose of their spacecraft.

Mari didn't move. "Red's right! We need food! We have to live!"

Jon reached out and pulled her after him as he moved out of the ship, balancing on the interwoven branches which supported the ship so precariously. He helped Mari gain an even footing on the thick bole of the tree, then motioned Red to follow.

The other man stepped onto the large branch, the small atomatic gun in his right hand.

Another ear-shattering snap exploded on the jungle air. The foliage shuddered as the ship slid downward again.

Red, still some feet away from the bole of the tree, weaved from side to side, struggling for balance. Then the ship slipped several more feet. Red suddenly swayed to the left. With a cry of rage and surprise, he was flung from the splintering branch.

As Red disappeared, Jon felt Mari slip off into empty space, her weight threatening to drag him off the branch with her.

CHAPTER TWO

Into the Jungle

If another branch had broken, if the ship had not come to a solid halt, Jon and Mari would have fallen some twenty feet to the ground, hitting against the branches in between. As it was, Jon had to fight for balance for some time before he could drag Mari back onto the branch.

A muffled curse sounded from below.

Relief burst through Jon. "You okay, Red?"

"Okay, hell! Almost busted in two!" Red sputtered. "Caught hold of a branch on my way down. Coulda been killed!"

Jon grinned at Mari. "Well, at least we're in one piece so far!"

Jon started to work his way down. With a little care it was possible to step down from branch to branch as if descending an insane staircase. Even Mari found the going fairly easy.

When Jon lowered the woman some six feet from the last branch, Red was there to grab her.

Jon dropped down next to his companions. They hadn't gone more than ten yards into the purple undergrowth before they heard a sudden crash.

Jon threw Mari to the ground and covered her body with his own. Red flattened behind thickly matted purplish ferns.

Jon held his breath as he felt the concussion. Then he rolled over and looked in the direction of the scout-boat. It was on the ground now—a twisted, shredded mass of metal,

17

ruined beyond repair.

Jon turned and examined the dark jungle, thick with creeping vines and flowery brush and ferns. The distant moans of strange animals growling, coughing, snarling, the odd soft chirping and singing of birds all patterned into a background murmuring that was forbiddingly alien. The planet's tropic sun burned dully through the interlaced overhanging trees. Insects buzzed in the underbrush but hung back as if afraid to attack these alien creatures from another world.

Jon pulled the atomatic gun from its holster at his side and motioned the others to follow. "We have to find water and a place to camp." They fell in line behind Jon; Mari first, Red pulling up at the end, holding his own atomatic gun.

For a long time Jon led them through the jungle, making his way around the trunks of gigantic trees which surrounded them at every turn, some of which were twelve feet thick at the base. The foliage was multicolored, ranging from the dark, almost blue-purple of the trees to the deeper purple color of the fern that matted the ground. Strangely shaped flowers of all colors splotched the vines and brush with flashes of alien beauty.

They had been traveling for some time before Mari asked tiredly, "Where are we going?"

"Have to find water," Jon answered briskly. "We'll need water and food."

"But we don't even know if we can drink the water!" Mari complained.

"Class-A planets have water, air, and natural food growing on their surface which will make human survival possible," he told her, as if quoting the book.

Mari was silent, but it was obvious she knew they could go on like this for days, finding nothing but thick underbrush and rotting vegetation.

Then suddenly they came upon a game trail packed solid by the hooves of nameless animals.

Red muttered his surprise and pleasure in such a way that his words were muffled under a large beefy hand.

Mari gasped. "People! Intelligent beings. This must lead to a city or...."

18

Jon's laugh cut her short. "That's made by wild game. And God only knows how dangerous they might be."

Then, sorry for dashing her hopes, Jon added: "But beasts cut natural paths through the jungle to a water hole— or a lake or river."

Mari asked, "Which way? Left or right?"

The three of them stood at the edge of the game trail which cut through the undergrowth in both directions like some long worm-like tunnel.

Jon finally bent down and examined some of the prints pressed into the matted jungle floor. "Look at these! At least a foot wide. Three-toed in front, four-toed behind. Clawed!"

Red moved for a closer look at the large marks. "Must be some beastie!"

"Hate to run up on this one in the old dark alley!" Jon grinned. But there was little humor in his voice. He rose slowly and turned to Mari. "We have to pick a direction and hope for the best."

"Does it really make much difference?" Mari asked flatly.

"Of course it matters!" Jon said sternly. "As long as we live it will matter. People have lived in conditions like these and survived. It happened on Verna, Tons, Yalli, Coriolla, just to name a few. Shipwrecked and... And beyond that, man came from a primitive beginning! So we can, if we make an effort. Now *you* pick a direction."

Mari nodded to the right and without a word Jon started off.

Like Mari's, his own thoughts were torn. A hard sense of defeat was impossible to ignore. Yet as a professional soldier he had fought under many conditions, on many planets—some jungle, others mountainous, airless worlds where temperatures ranged from far below at night to hellish boiling heat at day – and he had survived. Still, their present situation was different. There were no troops to land and join his own men. Here they were quite alone.

Making a turn in the tunnel-like game trail, Jon suddenly came face to face with an awful creature which might have come of some demon nightmare. What kept it from charging immediately, Jon didn't know.

19

Four legs supported the huge, thick-set body—short pillars not more than three feet. The thick, horny hide looked as hard as the steel plating on a rocket tube. Two small, helpless-looking arms hung just above the forward leg joints; eight thin, stringy fingers extended from the hand. Its back stood some ten feet high, arched in the middle to a large bony hump. The neck was corded with rippling muscles. The head, which hung low and forward almost on a level with Jon's, was long, cut in two by a huge, gaping mouth. A long, thin tongue darted in and out between stained purple teeth surrounded by red gums. Beady, red-rimmed eyes glared at him unblinkingly with almost human hatred.

The creature snorted and bellowed, then its short legs took several steps backward, kicking up twigs and loose leaves which were thick on the ground. Huge monstrous jaws opened wide, then snapped shut.

All this happened in the course of a few seconds, before the others had a chance to come around the curve. As Jon aimed his atomatic gun at the creature, a scream of terror came from Mari, followed by Red Fendricks low grunt of surprise.

Jon fired as the creature jerked forward in its murderous charge.

The impact of the pellet on the nose of the huge beast checked its forward motion. The pellet exploded, blowing away a good portion of the facial tissue and exposing the white jawbone. Jon fired again, and heard the whishing snap of Red's atomatic gun, firing to the right of him. The two atomic-charged pellets hit the animal almost at the same time—one in the shoulder and the other at the base of the brain. More of the creature's body shredded, exposing bloodied white bone, flesh, and oily light pink blood. The animal jerked back with each impact, then shuddered. It slowly slumped to the floor of the game trail, its muscles convulsing. Then it lay still.

Red shoved his gun into his belt and studied the creature for a moment. "There's an ugly one!"

Jon had turned to Mari. Her face was drained of color, but otherwise she seemed all right. Yet as Jon looked at her, he realized how helpless she really was—so young, so beautiful, so accustomed to comfort. Life since leaving the space liner must have been an unbearable strain on her nerves.

"Well, we survived that one," Jon said simply. But he was thinking hard. He had a little over fifty pellets strapped to his belt, with a fistful more in his pockets. That was all, and without them they wouldn't have a chance.

Jon searched the dead beast for any signs of moisture. He spotted mud caked on its front feet.

"If the mud means what I hope it does, water must be up ahead. Maybe some distance, though." Jon motioned the others to follow as he started off in the direction they had been going.

They continued on for some time, twisting and turning with the game trail. They were far more alert than before, prepared at every instant to find themselves facing some alien creature. It was a nerve-racking experience. As the minutes added up to hours, Jon felt the full strain on his body. Several times he looked back and saw the white tenseness of Mari's face. The woman could not last long without food, water and rest.

Several times they passed trees heavy with round, purple, juicy looking fruit which might be edible. But Jon was in no hurry to experiment. Once they had made camp and built a fire, he could then put the fruit to a simple test which would at least indicate whether it was worth taking a chance on tasting. According to the star chart rating, there should be plenty of food which they could eat and thrive upon.

* * * * * * *

Three hours had passed since killing the huge beast when they came to a point where the trail sloped steeply downward. They continued on, expecting to find water soon. Several times they heard creatures coming along the trail and quickly hid in the surrounding brush. Twice they came across beasts like the one they had killed. The creatures' movements were lumbering, almost awkward. Jon was sure that their brains were small. Their eyesight was quite bad;

21

their sense of smell couldn't have been much better, since the beasts passed within a few feet of their hiding place.

Once they came upon a slender animal with long, thin legs. Its purple fur was striped with black from shoulder to rump. The animal was not more than four feet at the shoulder, and its large eyes had the innocent appearance of a newborn baby. The animal took a long, careful look at them and then fled in the opposite direction.

"That looks like it might have good meat on it," Jon commented.

Red raised his gun too late. The little animal had disappeared around a turn in the trail.

A rustling in the bushes to their left brought them to a startled stop. Multicolored birds fluttered into the game trail. Then a group of small, six-legged, furry creatures with greenish hides sprang out of the bushes, scampered across the trail and disappeared.

Jon grinned. "Getting closer to a collection of animal life."

Red nodded but said nothing. Mari's eyes brightened hopefully. The men shared her relief. Water meant life, hope for survival. And they needed hope almost as much as food and water.

They continued down the game trail for a few hundred feet and then came to a turn which twisted abruptly to the left.

As they started in this new direction, the soft sound of rippling water came to their ears.

They rushed blindly forward. After half a dozen running steps, Jon came to a sudden stop.

Not fifty feet away was the bank of a river some ten to fifteen feet wide.

Mari laughed happily. "Fellas, I'm going to have a swim and a bath!"

* * * * * * *

Mari hummed as she slowly slipped out of her clothing behind a bush. All thoughts of the danger which faced them faded as she listened to the singing of the tropical birds, the

22

bubbling rhythm of the small river, and the muffled conversation of the two men some twenty feet away.

She now felt as safe with Jon and Red as she would with her father and brother.

Mari slipped into the cool waters, thrilling to the soothing effect they had on her tired muscles. Her thoughts wandered to her past life, so different from what she now faced.

All she had known was the protection of a rich family, traveling across the Galactic Federation, seeing different kinds of worlds. But it had been an impersonal childhood, with Interstellar Tele-Teachers giving her an education until the age of twenty; after that she went to college to obtain personalized instruction. All had been a means of training her for a position in life which was hardly expected to be wonderfully happy. As the daughter of Dorna Enterprises, she had a duty to live a life mapped out in every detail.

Thoughts of her childhood and its unhappy memories turned now to the present and her immediate situation. A shudder rushed through her, and she fought off an emotional burst of tears.

Then Mari remembered Jon and Red. The two men were completely different from those she had met as the daughter of a rich man. Jon Handon was the professional soldier. She had heard strange stories of these men who fought at the outer frontiers of the Federation, living with death every day and then escaping into the barrooms in the cheaper sections of space-port towns which catered to their every whim and desire. Mari had been taught that such men were beasts who did not respect a woman's honor, who came from the lower levels of society and were below contempt. Yet Jon Handon had been a gentleman. Never once had he offered her harm, even if his eyes had betrayed his interest many times in the past days.

Red was something different again.

Mari grinned as her spirits lifted. The two men believed she knew nothing of the crude words which Red attempted to hold back. They didn't expect a woman of her class to know anything about life.

Mari puzzled over her sudden change of mood, for it

23

seemed so unreasonable. Every muscle had ached, her nerves had been on the verge of giving away with every step they had taken that day. Yet, upon seeing the river, seeing water and realizing what it meant, Mari had felt her spirits lift fantastically, and hope had returned.

And there was another reason to feel momentarily lifted from the depression of defeat, because what surrounded her now was a garden of beauty.

Mari swam out toward the middle of the river. A rock and sand bottom glistened below the crystal water. On shore the trees were sprinkled with the multicolored flowers and twining vines. There was nothing ugly about the jungle itself. This was a paradise lovelier than anything she had seen in all her travels.

A splashing sound came from behind her, from the shore. Mari turned, and stared in sheer terror at what she saw coming toward her.

Her lips opened wide. A horror-filled scream cut through the late afternoon jungle air; she beat the water with her arms, just barely keeping her head above its surface as her eyes glazed over with shock.

CHAPTER THREE

Captives

Red and Jon were gathering some fern branches for bedding when the blood-curdling scream broke the jungle silence.

The two men burst into a run and reached the river bank almost together, atomatic guns at the ready. At first all they saw was the screaming girl in the middle of the river. Then Jon suddenly spotted a brownish, shiny head on the surface of the water, going toward her.

Without a moment's hesitation, Jon lifted his right arm, pointed the small hand weapon at the fast-moving, slimy head, and fired. The action appeared to be one careless move, a snap shot; yet as the gun fired, an explosive charge struck the reptile like monster.

The torn remains of the huge head reared upward some five feet upon a long, slender neck; a hideous scream came from the gaping fang-lined mouth. The elongated body slowly lifted upward from the water and then splashed sideways as a second explosive pellet struck it from Jon's gun.

Mari was still screaming as the scaled animal disappeared downstream, quite dead, whipping over and over in the waters. Not until the creature had finally sunk from sight did she stop screaming.

Then, like a person pursued by demons, she started swimming toward the shore.

Jon and Red stood guard until Mari had reached a point

25

of safety within a few feet of the shore, then they reluctantly turned so that she could gain the dry land without having to reveal her nudity to them.

After some minutes, Jon heard footsteps behind them.

"Are you all right?"

For a moment there was no answer, then Mari's voice half whispered from directly behind Jon. "I think so."

The two men turned as one and faced the now fully clothed young woman. She was trembling, white-faced, looking from one man to the other.

"Thanks," she finally said in a strangely weak voice. "I thought..."

Then, without warning, Mari slumped to the ground, unconscious.

Jon lifted her gently and carried her to their campsite. He lowered her onto some of the half-finished bedding.

"She all right?" Red rasped.

Jon nodded. "Some shock. She's been wonderful. This has been pretty hard on all of us—but she's a woman. I don't see how she makes it!"

Mari moaned and opened her eyes. She looked up at Jon. For a moment she seemed about to cry, then her jaw set more firmly and she started to sit up. Jon reached down and took her hand.

"I'm sorry," Mari said, standing. But the tone of her voice implied that she would not let anything let that happen again. "We'd better make camp!"

Jon wanted to tell Mari that there was nothing wrong with fainting, or screaming, or being frightened out of her wits. He wanted to tell her how brave she was—how much she had amazed both of them. But he said nothing, merely watching her start to gather fern for their bedding.

* * * * * * *

Some hours later the sun had lowered to the horizon, bringing almost total darkness. Their campfire dimly illuminated the immediate surroundings. There was a small pile of twigs and dried leaves beside the fire, from which they could feed the flames when necessary. All three were huddled around the warming fire. Jon was handling some of the purple fruit which he had picked and brought to camp a short time before.

"I'll throw one of these on the fire. See how it reacts to heat. A bad test, I'll admit, but better than nothing. Watch it burn, smell the fumes." As he spoke, Jon tossed one of the fruits onto the fire; it lay there gathering heat from the flames.

"What will that prove?" Mari asked.

Jon looked into her face, beautifully outlined in the flickering firelight. "Well, if it reacts to heat in the same manner as most fruit we know, we'll at least have some small indication where to go from there."

"I don't get it," Red grumbled.

"Put it this way," Jon reasoned. "If it reacts unexpectedly, like exploding or bubbling like thick oil, then we don't take any unnecessary chances. If it smells strange, or the fumes have an effect on us, then we forget it. If it just lays there and cooks like any known fruit might, then we have at least narrowed things down."

"Sounds risky to me!" Red exclaimed.

While waiting for the fruit to react to the heat, Jon surveyed their immediate surroundings. They had picked a fairly open place along the river bank. At this point the area was grassy for fifteen feet in all directions. They had comfortable bedding for the night, made from the lacy fern leaves so common to the area and so easily broken from the plants.

Beyond some seventy atomatic pellets, their clothing and Jon's knowledge of planetary survival which had been successfully drilled into him at Basic Training for the Space Service, they were quite defenseless against the alien world in which they were trapped. But no more so than their savage ancestors, who had survived in jungles on Mother Earth. The complex society which evolved finally took man to the stars, to span the galaxy with two huge Federations—which had been at war with each other for more than a hundred years.

Jon looked down at the purple fruit in the fire and grinned. It was slowly cooking. The skin had stretched and broken, exposing a white, pulpy fruit which was already beginning to turn brown.

He looked at the other two. "Well, now for the final experiment. The taste test!"

Just as Jon reached for one of the purple fruits, they were alerted by a soft humming which was rapidly coming closer.

"What is it?" Mari whispered.

Jon motioned her quiet. Then a slow grin spread across his face as the roaring became louder and nearer.

"It's one of the scout-boats!" he shouted, standing. "One of them made it!"

He pulled the atomatic gun from its holster. Quickly he jerked the timer, automatically rupturing a small cap in the atomic pellet in the firing chamber. Then, raising the gun and pointing it into the sky, he squeezed the trigger.

A few seconds later, light exploded some thousand feet in the sky.

"Let's hope they see it!" Jon said.

The distant roar was now beginning to fade. For some time he stood there, arms at his sides, defeated. Whoever had been in the scout-boat had not noticed the distress flare, a universally known signal.

"Well," Jon sighed, "we know that at least there are other human beings on this planet. They'll land somewhere. We'll find them."

"What now?" Mari asked, looking up at him.

"Tomorrow we'll start out after them. They're landed. I'd say, a score or fifty miles and they hit ground. A distress signal when we are closer could bring us together. Their ship is probably in one piece, too. The radio beam will bring help." Jon tried to make his voice sound hopeful. "Then it will be only a matter of time before finally returning home."

Mari's face brightened. "Do you think we can find them? Do you really believe it?"

"Sure!" Red blurted. "What you talkin' about?"

"Sure, we're gonna find them!"

But Jon knew that the other man had also figured their chances were slim. If Mari noticed the fact, she showed no outward sign. Her face was bright and smiling, her large blue eyes glittering in the firelight.

They would find the other ship—if it had landed within twenty miles, if it had not made a crash landing, if it was possible to survive the days of marching distance between. And if the purple fruit proved edible.

With that last thought, Jon took a small bite of the fruit in his hand, letting the juicy material lay on his tongue.

The other two held their breaths.

Slowly the flavor was picked up by his tongue. Its pleasant, sweet taste was completely new to Jon, but quite enjoyable.

Jon swallowed, then after a few seconds he smiled. "Well, I guess we'll live. If it's not a slow poison."

He was about to tell the others to wait, but they were already taking quick bites from the fruit they had been holding while awaiting his judgment.

Jon shrugged and took another bite. Chances were they would likely face another day and then another, until death, in some form, caught up with them.

An hour passed before Jon was satisfied that the fruit was not only pleasant to eat, but perfectly harmless to human beings.

By that time he was lying on his back, feet pressed close to the warming fire, darkness blanketing the sky. He lay there for some time, finding it hard to sleep. His thoughts centered on Mari. He wished there were some way to send her back home where she belonged.

After setting foot on the jungle floor that morning, Jon had given their chances of survival a flat zero. Yet they had managed to make it through the day, to find water and a safe food substance. Maybe their luck would hold out.

With that thought, Jon fell asleep. The next thing he knew, Red was shaking his shoulder.

"Time for you to be takin' watch!"

Jon sat up, fed the fire, and then huddled close, atomatic gun ready in his right hand. He listened to the night sounds of the jungle. The near and distant noises of unseen animals sent chills through him. Once he saw a burning pair of eyes staring at him from across the river.

Jon sat there and thought about himself and Mari and Red. Three people who under normal circumstances would never have known each other, but now depended upon one another for survival and companionship. Red, raised in a tough city, of questionable business activities. Mari, young and used to the soft life of the very rich. And himself, a professional soldier. Yet each of them had the one element common to all living creatures: the need and will to survive, to continue no matter how bad things got. For the first time in his life, the war which had been continuing between the two Galactic Federations seemed quite distant and unimportant.

It wasn't until the sky began to color with dim light that Jon's thoughts turned to the immediate necessity of facing their second day on this world.

He woke the others and was just passing out the morning fruit supply when suddenly a half dozen piercing yells sounded from just beyond the thick wall of jungle growth which surrounded the small clearing.

As Jon grabbed for his atomatic gun, the foliage parted in a dozen places. Spear-carrying, human-like forms rushed out, swarming over the three helpless Citizens of the Federation.

It all happened so fast that Jon didn't even have a chance to fight. He was crushed under the weight of several bodies. A hard object hit him on the side of the head and consciousness snapped.

The next thing Jon knew, he was lying on his back, his head resting against the trunk of a tree. For some moments he didn't move. He listened to the chattering voices which seemed to surround him. That they sounded human seemed incredible. He could remember seeing shaggy, hairy, almost naked forms charging at him. For one instant before awareness snapped off like a rocket tube gone dead, a bearded face had loomed large over his head. If not human, there was every chance that the creature was some distant cousin, some evolutionary offshoot. At least a humanoid.

Red's voice interrupted his thoughts. "Them creatures— dirty sin-mots! They're human if I ever seen humans!"

"How could they be?" Mari asked in a small voice.

Jon opened his eyes and turned toward the voices. "Where are we?"

"Are you all right?" Mari asked gently. Her head was the only thing that moved as she looked at him. Like Red and himself, her hands were bound behind her. "I thought that maybe..."

Jon suddenly realized he was not in the clearing where they had camped the night before. "What happened?"

"They carried you," Red quickly informed him.

"How long have I been out?" Jon was painfully aware of a lump at the side of his head.

"About an hour or so," Red answered.

"Where have they been taking us? What direction?"

Before Red could reply, one of their half-naked captors stepped up, grunted and prodded him with the point of a spear. It was the first time Jon had a chance to get a good look at one of them. The man standing over him, holding the primitive spear in his huge hands was thickly bearded, with long hair falling over his shoulders. He wore a loin cloth, made of some animal hide, around his middle. Otherwise he was naked. The only thing which showed any improvement over a caveman level was the point of the spear. It was of hard metal, and gleamed, razor sharp. For some moments Jon stared at the spear point, puzzled

Then the man spoke to him, pricking the spear into his leg. "Yoöp! Žésst Yoöp!"

Jon immediately understood the meaning of the spear jab, but it took him some seconds to realize that the words sounded vaguely understandable. He didn't have a chance to say anything to the others about this until all three had been forced to their feet and pushed along the trail.

Mari was walking just in front of Jon. She turned. "I could swear he said for us to get up!"

Her voice held more amazement than fear. Apparently it did not really occur to her that they were in danger. Jon decided not to point it out.

He nodded. "I was thinking the same thing."

One of their guards hit Jon with the butt of his spear, and muttered something which sounded like "Shut up!"

They continued on in silence.

Jon studied their surroundings, basically unchanged since he had first seen the jungle. His gaze fell on Mari's legs. There was nothing he could do about escaping right then; it was best to think of something else. Anything, even Mari's beauty. But as time went on, his mind wandered over his life, the long battles which had been fought for the glory of the Federation. Strangely, everything in that existence already seemed dreamlike, as if it had happened to another man. All the battles and all the women in the cheap bars were now unreal.

Jon forced his thoughts into focus. Apparently their captors were human. This could be a world on which human colonies had formed and degenerated to a savage culture. Or a planet where some liner had crashed, only to be lost forever, forgotten. The fact that their language sounded much like a mutation of his own seemed to indicate that they were the descendants of a past space wreck or small colony.

Still, all this brought little hope. Even if he could make them understand that it was to their benefit to help Mari, Red and himself find one of the scout-boats, they would not take his plea seriously. Primitive people hated and distrusted strangers. Generally a stranger was killed immediately—or enslaved.

Jon had no idea how long they continued down the game trail before turning and taking a well-marked narrow pathway which had apparently been cut by human hand. He saw a clearing ahead, then all at once they were standing before a primitive village made up of small thatched huts and surrounded by a spiked fence of logs some seven feet high. Around the wall was a series of sharpened spikes, aimed outward at a forty-degree angle. These were placed about a foot apart and circled the wall six deep. It was a simple but effective protection against the beasts of the jungle.

Jon, Mari and Red were pushed through open gates which immediately closed behind them and their captors.

Jon felt a sharp jab at the small of his back and he moved at once toward the tiny bullet-shaped hut as the savage had directed him. Mari and Red followed, in front of two other guards.

The three of them were pushed into the hut, then the thick leathery flap which hung from the door frame was lashed tightly shut. The hut itself was made of packed dirt, supported by crude wooden framing.

Jon pushed against the flimsy-looking door, but the leathery substance was far tougher than it looked. The material merely stretched slightly against the pressure.

Jon turned and faced his companions, grinning helplessly. "Well, just wondered."

The small hut was almost totally dark. What little light there was filtered through the seams of the leather door. Mari and Red were huddled in the middle of the hut.

"What are they going to do with us?" Mari sounded weak and frightened.

"I don't know." Jon wished he could say something comforting, but he could not lie to her. Death might be quite close. He believed everybody had the right to face their last minutes without false hopes.

Red grunted and moved away from them, leaning against the curving wall of the hut. "You ask me, it just might be easier to be killed. Ain't nothin' we can do about it anyway!"

"We can try!" Mari snapped, much to Jon's amazement. "I've given a lot of thought to what you said yesterday about us continuing, Jon. We have only one life. If it is going to be taken and we don't try to fight for it, then we deserve to die!"

"How we goin' to fight with our hands tied?" Red asked, looking to Jon for the answer.

"Well, if they aren't going to starve us to death, they'll have to untie our hands."

A blinding light flared as one of their captors stepped into the hut. The man carried a large bowl. He placed it on the ground in the middle of the hut and started to leave.

Jon shouted: "Wait! We're tied!"

The other whipped around and started to move forward threateningly. Jon managed to work himself around so that his bound hands were visible.

The man laughed, then moved to Mari and quickly untied her. A moment later the two men were also free.

After the savage left and tied down the door, the three moved to the bowl. It was filled with greasy meat and some pale vegetables. In the semi-darkness of the hut they could just barely make out the dull colors and shapes.

"Doesn't smell bad," Mari admitted.

"Ain't good, either!" Red grunted.

"It's food," Mari pointed out bravely. "And I'm starved."

Jon's heart burst with pride at her words. "Well, let's give it a try!"

Mari made a face. "I guess we eat with our hands."

"There ain't nothin' else we can do, Mari!" Red's tone was gruff but gentle.

Mari hesitated for only a moment, then reached into the bowl with her right hand and pulled out a lump of coarse meat.

Jon and Red quickly followed her example.

Jon swallowed and finally broke the silence. "Not bad, considering…"

Mari shuddered and dipped into the bowl once more. They ate hungrily, in turns, until most of the contents of the bowl had disappeared. It was a sweet-tasting meat. The vegetables were soft and pulpy, much like Earth potatoes.

After they had finished, Mari looked at her greasy hands for a long time. Then she wiped her hands on the sides of her slacks. "I guess we'll have to go native!"

Her statement triggered sudden laughter. All three of them doubled over, finding relief from their fears in the unexpected and humorous irony of her words.

Their near-hysterical laughter sounded in the small confines of the hut until the door flap opened and a guard threatened them with his spear.

"S'qiàté!" the savage shouted.

This time there was no question as to what he had said, and the captives immediately fell silent.

The man motioned with his spear. "Shüm!"

The three stood and stepped out of the hut. They were immediately surrounded by half a dozen warriors who pushed them toward the far side of the village.

Jon's mind was spinning with theories about the language of these people. It seemed so much like his own, but with a difference. Could it be a degenerate form of the Galactic language, he wondered. But he had no chance to ponder the question for long.

They were taken to a large clearing at the back of the village. There a monstrously fat old man was sitting on a mud dais which served as some kind of throne. His body was covered from head to foot with grease. He was naked except for a g-string around his middle.

They were shoved in front of the man, who glared at them as if they were some kind of prize animals just brought from market for his approval.

Jon pulled Mari closer to him. He half expected her to move away, but instead she seemed to hug even nearer.

An exchange followed between their head guard—one of the men who had originally captured them—and the man in front of them. Finally the fat man turned and pointed. "Tår!"

The captives were pushed back to the hut then. But instead of ordering them inside, one of the guards moved between Mari and the men.

Mari paled with horror as the two men were shoved and prodded across the village and toward the outer gate.

All Jon could think of was that the savages were planning something terrible and degenerate for Mari. Every nerve ached to fight for freedom, but there was nothing he could do against a whole village of armed savages. There was nothing he could do for Mari but die—and that would serve no purpose at all.

Then suddenly they were shoved out through the gate and Jon could see Mari no more.

THE SLAVES OF LOMOORO, BY CHARLES NUETZEL

CHAPTER FOUR

The Raiders

The guards forced them toward the open gate and into the clearing beyond. Red turned. "Where you think they're takin' us?"

"I don't know. But what about Mari?" Jon fought the lump tightening in his throat. "If they so much as touch her..."

"Yeah!" Red grunted.

They were shoved around the walled village until they found themselves facing a large plowed field being worked by half a dozen male slaves. Three guards with spears and whips stood watch over them.

"You see that?" Red exclaimed. "Look at them!"

Jon was as surprised as the other man. Farming was the last thing he would have guessed his captors able to handle.

The furrows in the soft earth were not quite straight, but nevertheless were obviously irrigation ditches. The field extended some twenty feet in each direction. Beyond it was the jungle's barrier wall of vegetation.

"Verdà!" one of their guards ordered. "Verdà!"

They were shoved to the field. In moments the guards had shown them how to pick the small berries from the thorny plants growing there.

Jon had only a moment to take notice of their fellow workers, but that was enough to suggest startling conclusions. These men were dressed in form-fitting slacks; their shirts opened in front. The material of the clothing was finely woven, though now faded and tattered from wear.

The implications whirled in Jon's brain. The tribesmen were not the only humans on this planet, nor were they the most advanced.

The tribesmen worked their slaves all during the hot day, allowing them to rest only when the sun had reached the center of the sky. Then they were fed much the same kind of food they had eaten that morning.

This was Jon's first chance to see his fellow prisoners more closely. They appeared to be refined and intelligent. All were bearded to some degree, but their beards were not as long and shaggy as their captors'.

One of the prisoners who had only a short growth of beard attracted Jon's immediate attention. The man was blonde, like himself, and his muscular body moved with the grace of a dancer. There was that about the man which suggested the professional soldier. Jon studied him more carefully. The man worked completely alone, ate alone, and spoke only when spoken to.

There was little chance to communicate with fellow prisoners at this time. As they ate, the guards kept careful watch, ready to hit anyone who spoke.

After the meal they were forced back to work, filling the small leather bags given them by the guards.

Jon was exhausted at the end of the day. The awkward bending had cramped every muscle in his body. Several times when he had hesitated too long during the last hours, one of the guards had slashed a leather whip across his back.

Jon and Red were marched with the other slave-prisoners back to the village, but this time were taken to a different hut.

All the male slaves were put in a large hut. Just before he entered it, Jon looked around. If Mari was anywhere in the village, he could not see her.

Depressed, exhausted, sick inside, Jon folded up against the wall, trying not to think about Mari. But it was obvious that she had begun to mean a lot to him. More than he wanted her to mean. Mari was helpless. But for that matter they were all helpless. Without weapons, they were safer here in the village. All that was left was the ammunition in

38

their belts.

When the guards brought food, Jon hardly touched the community bowl. He could not stop worrying about Mari. He ate only out of necessity. After dinner he slipped down against the wall of the hut and shut his eyes.

* * * * * *

It took Jon several days to overcome his depression. During that time he merely existed, working as ordered. Red seemed to adjust to the situation without any outward sign of strain except for an unaccustomed and silent solemnity.

The young blonde captive approached Jon on the second evening, during their night meal. He smiled and said something which was almost understandable.

"I'm sorry," Jon managed, shrugging his shoulders.

The man grinned and pointed to himself. "Tanín. Misa Tanín." Then he pointed to Jon.

Jon forced a grin and said his own name.

"Jon, Tanín. Jon, Tanín," the other announced, pointing from Jon to himself and back, using the right word in each case.

At that point the guard came in to take the empty food bowl, and ordered them to silence.

Jon curled up against the wall. It was a long time before he fell asleep.

The next day, when they were on their way back to the prison hut, Jon learned the answer to his question about Mari's welfare. He saw her in the village square where they had been "interviewed" by the tribe's chief. She was tending a fire. At sight of her, his heart leaped. It was all he could do to keep from running to her and throwing his arms around that dear form to let her know how relieved he was that she was alive and apparently safe.

Then the guards forced him into the prison hut.

"You see her?" Jon asked Red. "Yeah!" Red was grinning from ear to ear.

* * * * * * *

Every night since being separated from Jon and Red, Mari had tried to catch their attention when they were passed into the slave hut. When Mari saw Jon turn her way, she sighed with relief.

At least they knew she was alive. Ever since seeing her two companions pushed away at spear-point on their first day in the village, Mari had been frightened and sick inside. She had believed that the savage brutes planned on using her for a plaything. But much to her surprise, they merely put her to work helping the other female slaves fix the evening meal. She was given the same hut as before, but other female slaves spent the nights there with her. Mari had tried to make friends with the others, but they kept to themselves and ignored her.

The first two nights she rolled and tossed. Dreams of such horror tormented her sleep that she awoke several times, screaming. One dream haunted her all the next day. In that dream she had been chased by monstrous beasts of the jungle. Jon and Red stood by, ignoring her. She had run to Jon, only to have him shove her brutally aside. "Please, Jon, please. Help me! I love you—I love you!" When she awoke, her mind rebelled, for Jon Handon was the last person in the universe she could love. He was a professional killer. A soldier, a brute, not much above the savages of this village.

Yet as Mari saw Jon turn toward her that evening, she felt her heart leap.

Now Mari put a branch under the cook pot and watched as the flames licked the wood. Once more she felt hopeless depression. Death would be far better than slavery for the rest of her life in this little village. Somehow they would have to escape, or she would kill herself.

Then the mood passed at the thought of Jon Handon. As long as he lived, there was hope for all of them. She was sure of that.

* * * * * * *

During the evening meal, Jon moved to Tanín and smiled. "How about us being friends?" He spoke the words very slowly and carefully, hoping that some of their meaning would filter through.

"Tanín, Jon—friends," he said a moment later when it was apparent that the other did not understand.

Tanín suddenly grinned. "Fräyíndès."

The meaning was obvious and Jon laughed with relief. He called Red over and pointed to him, repeating his name.

In minutes the three were beginning serious attempts to communicate. After some trouble, Jon made it clear that he wished to learn Tanín's language. Once that had been established, Tanín began the painful process of teaching both of them.

In the next days they made rapid progress. Although both languages had the same root, there were meanings of common words, which had changed. At first their exchanges were limited to "Good morning" and "Good night," but as the days slipped by, Jon began to pick up enough words to carry on a conversation of sorts with Tanín.

Their knowledge was quickly advanced one day when a huge tropic storm, like the one which had greeted their arrival on the planet, kept them confined to the hut. There they spent the long hours learning more of the world's common language.

After the storm passed, they worked hard in the fields. Sometimes they went out into the jungle to gather special roots and bring in animals caught in the tribe's primitive traps. Slowly Jon began to get a picture of the tribal life of their captors. Basically they lived by hunting and gathering their food from the jungles. They had learned something about farming and making fairly hard metals to fashion their spear points. Most labor was done by slaves, while the men of the tribe lived comfortable existences, hunting and drinking their *pro tias,* a form of liquor fermented from the berries which Jon and his fellow prisoner-slaves picked when ripe.

The meat which the tribe used, Jon discovered, was from the *Norti.* Jon and his two companions had seen this kind of animal during their first day on the planet. It was the slender, long legged striped creature which had run away from them when Red had attempted to shoot it. Jon learned that its purple hide was used to make the loin cloths worn by the

41

tribesmen.

He saw Mari several times, usually in the evening around the camp's cook fire. But they were never close enough to communicate except by gestures.

As he learned more of the language from Tanín, he began to ask probing questions about the world on which they were now slaves.

Tanín called the world Lomooro, and said he came from a city named Tal-Jaÿ, which was many marches from the village of the Rals—the name by which he called their savage masters.

"In time my people should miss me. They will come searching. Then, when they rescue me, we will go to Tal-Jaÿ and you will be honored as a guest of our people," Tanín told Jon one night. "I am honored there as Warrior Lord, my uncle being High Captain, of Royal birth, descendant of the first High Captain."

When Jon questioned Tanín about the origin of his people, Tanín replied: "From here—from Lomooro!"

"Who was the first High Captain?" Jon asked.

"Legend has it that he was a god who came from the sky." Tanín shrugged his broad shoulders.

"What does legend tell?" Jon persisted.

"Surely you know from where we all came. Everybody on Lomooro knows!"

"I am from far away," Jon said. "From a place you would not understand."

"That truly must be far."

"What does the legend say?" Jon leaned closer.

"That God First High Captain came from the skies in a large city with many of his sub-gods and sub-goddesses and they picked this world to live on. They stayed here and bred children and created all the beauty of our world. They warred with the Rals and..."

"The Rals were here first?"

"So it says in the Book. There are many books which tell of the first High Captain. If you ever get back to Tal-Jaÿ, I will show them to you."

"What else does the book say?" Jon's mind was already swimming with theories.

Tanín grinned and spoke in a solemn mocking voice:

> And lo, there came upon the ground the city of Gods.
> And lo, it was beautiful and perfect. And lo, God High Captain begat the sons of God and they became the fathers of our cities.
> And lo, those sons of God and fathers of cities warred upon one another and upon the savages of the jungle,
> And lo, they would not look upon each other again!

Tanín shrugged. "And that is the beginning of our Holy High Captain's *Book of Lomooro*!"

"How long ago did all this happen?"

"As long as recorded history and then back further to the beginning of time," Tanín announced with authority.

"And how many cities are there?"

"Many," Tanín explained. In the conversation which followed, Jon listened as more details were offered by his new friend, Tanín of Tal-Jaÿ.

There were many cities on Lomooro, two of which were Tal-Jaÿ and Nal-Iò. Tanín had little real knowledge of his world, believing that the continent was in itself the whole world, floating on an endless sea of water dotted with only a few offshore islands.

When Jon tried to explain the true state of the universe and Lomooro, that what they stood on was merely one of several such continents on a world which in turn was round like a ball, Tanín only shook his head sadly. He was unable to understand.

"You talk like our First High Captain's stories for children. They make no sense. And you make even less!"

Lomooro was a place of savage beasts, countless tribes of primitive Rals like the ones of this village, Tanín explained. "And, like the beasts, we all eat upon one another. Tal-Jaÿ is always at war with the other walled cities. And everybody is at war with the Rals. The Raiders are at war with everyone else. I was on a march with a patrol of Tal-Jaÿ troops, attempting to find a hunting party which had not returned to the city, when we were attacked by Raiders. In the battle all of my men were killed, along with the last of the Raiders. I started back for Tal-Jaÿ and not two days later I was captured by these Rals." Tanín shrugged. "So here I am, former Warrior Lord, now a slave of the Rals."

As Jon understood it, Lomooro was a loosely knit civilization held together by bickering wars and Raiders who took prisoners from one city or from the Rals and sold them to another city for trade goods or Tals—metal tokens which had trading value accepted in all the cities. It was a primitive social development, if that. According to Tanín, the most advanced weapons were swords and bows and arrows. Explosives were unknown.

That night, lying in the darkness, Jon suddenly remembered the explosive pellets. He had thought them useless without his atomatic gun, but now his fingers checked his holster and the fifty atomic charged pellets which were attached. With a sharp pointed object, he could puncture the soft time caps on their sides and within a few moments they would blow up—a perfect weapon to throw terror into the hearts of the primitive men of Lomooro.

It was then that he decided to talk to Tanín about the possibility of escaping as a group, and whether there was much chance of their getting to the city of Tal-Jaÿ.

The next morning Jon was startled awake by the terrified scream of Ral warriors. Immediately everybody in the hut came to their feet. Jon moved to Tanín. "What do you make of it?"

Tanín slowly shook his head.

A high-pitched yell, a war chant, came to their ears.

"Raiders!" said one of the other prisoners. Tanín nodded.

Jon asked: "Won't they take you back to your home? To Tal-Jaÿ?"

Tanín shook his head grimly. "Not a chance. If they did, my people would slay as many of them as possible and torture those captured, and refuse to do business with the survivors. No, they will take me to Nal-Iò, or some other nearby city. Probably Nal-Iò, since it is closer."

"But surely your people know that the Raiders take their people and sell them into slavery to the other cities and..."

Tanín spoke with a tinge of irony. "To know is one thing, to have it spit in our faces is another! The Raiders are smart. They work as a news service between cities. They will even smuggle presents to slaves from their families, if paid well. Whatever will bring them profit—but in the long run. There is an ethic they follow, and if they were to break it, their business would crumble."

Tanín shook his head again. "No, my friend, we are about to go from simple labor to the more complex form of slavery in the City. And there is nothing we can do about it."

Jon thought of his gun belt filled with atomatic pellets, and immediately tried to picture it in the eyes of some primitive slaver. Such a belt with those "pretty stones" would seem a treasure, something different, that could be sold to the highest bidder. He immediately removed the belt, detached the holster which had been hooked on by magnetic clamps, and then reversed the belt so that it showed only a smooth inner surface.

Red grinned. "I got some of them in my pockets."

Before Jon could reply, there was a loud crash outside the village, followed by yells and screams from Ral warriors.

"What'll they do?" Jon asked, turning to Tanín. "Enslave the whole village?"

Suddenly a guard broke into the hut. "Come!" the man ordered, threatening them with his spear. "Come!"

One by one the prisoners walked out of the hut. To Jon's surprise, all resistance had ended. Several Ral warriors lay on the ground, arrows in their dead bodies. The village gate was wide open and a line of men mounted on strange, slender beasts was entering the village.

* * * * * * *

Jon saw them only briefly, for he and the other prisoners were pushed toward the back of the village, to the Ral chieftain. But what he saw was startling enough.

The warriors were clothed in long colored robes and had leathery quivers of arrows strapped to their backs. About the

45

middle of each man was a belt from which hung a long, curving sword and a slender knife. All but their leader held a spear and bow.

Their mounts were blue, sway-backed, and had remarkably large heads. Their sharp teeth were evenly spaced. But there was a gentleness in the creatures' eyes which looked almost sadly human. Long fur covered the complete beast, except at the three-toed hooves. A long, hairless tail extended out behind the animals, ending in a bushy tip. Jon remembered that Tanín had called the native Lomoorian mount a *Martos.*

The spears which the Raiders held were more like lances, having long, sword-like points which looked razor sharp and seemed to be used as much for slicing and hacking as for thrusting. All the warriors were bearded and most of them were dark haired. Unlike the Rals, who were dirty and primitive in their personal habits, the Raiders had well-groomed faces. Everything about them looked neat, sharp and intelligent. Their colorful clothing was sleek and attractive.

Jon heard his name whispered from behind as they were herded into the clearing in front of the chief. He turned and found Mari standing a foot away.

"Are you all right?" he quickly asked.

"Yes." Then she giggled. "You look funny with the beard."

It was the first time Jon had considered his appearance. He had not shaved during his captivity. He fingered his beard and grinned.

There was no time for any further exchange. The Raider who had come in at the head of the column of riders was more finely dressed, with a headpiece made of shiny blue metal which fitted over his head like a crooked bowl. He dismounted in front of the grossly fat Chief of the Rals.

"I came for slaves," the man announced. "Bal-jan-dà, Chief of the Jan-dà Raiders, commands all your slaves and one out of ten of your people, or he will burn down your village and take all the women and children to hang on the points of his spears! One man out of ten, and two..." Bal-jan-dà hesitated, eyeing the Chief of the Rals. Then an oily grin spread across his features. "Five women!"

The Chief blubbered slightly for a moment, his eyes growing large. Then he raised a huge bloated arm. "You rob me. But...it shall be as you desire!"

THE SLAVES OF LOMOORO, BY CHARLES NUETZEL

CHAPTER FIVE

Lorn-jan-dà

Bal-jan-dà turned and faced the group in which Jon and his companions were standing. "There are the prisoners—your slaves? All of them?"

"Yes, yes!" the Ral Chief grunted. "Take them and leave. Take what you want. Leave us in peace."

Bal-jan-dà nodded. "Line up all your women, all your men, and I will pick those who will come with us."

Jon saw no more, for some of the Jan-dà Raiders herded his group away from the village and beyond the wall. Jon did manage to keep Mari and Tanín close to him. Though they had spoken no words, it seemed that his Lomooro friend was happy to stay nearby.

They formed into a long line, then one of the Raiders came with a long rope to which metal loops were attached at intervals of three feet. One of these loops was closed around the neck of each prisoner.

Jon managed to get Mari in front of him. Tanín came after him, then Red. He would have wished Red to be in front of Mari. Then they were ordered to sit down and wait.

The moment they had settled themselves Tanín said: "I know Bal-jan-dà well. He has come to our home and done business for many years with my family. He is hard to do business with, but a good and just man."

Jon jumped at that tiny straw of hope. "Then maybe after all there's a chance to talk him into..."

Tanín's laughter cut Jon short. "No, my friend! These

are even more reasons he will *not* do more than tell my family where I am. He will say he saw me in Nal-Iò. Nothing more." Tanín shrugged. "This is life. We have to make the best of it. Who are we to change things which have been for all of time?"

Jon nodded toward Mari, ignoring the temptation to argue Tanín's last point. "What about her? What will they do to her?"

"She will be sold to some man as a slave woman to share his bed at night." Tanín grinned as he looked at Mari. For a moment he said nothing, studying her strange civilized clothing. It was now soiled and torn, but she looked amazingly neat. "She would make a wonderful slave. What a woman to have at your command!"

Jon fought down irritation. He was glad that Mari did not speak Lomoorian. "Is there nothing I can do..?"

"If she already had a man. Only if mated. Then she would be sold to the same Master as her mate. We are not savages. We will not split a mated couple."

Jon leaped at this, not even considering Mari's reaction. "She is my mate!"

Tanín's eyes narrowed. "If she is your mate, then make sure everybody knows it!"

Jon expected to make full use of the warning. He was about to tell Mari his plans when some of the Raiders came up with a dozen more prisoners to be bound to the line behind Red. When he started to talk to Mari, one of the Raiders ordered him to be silent.

Jon felt as if he had been pushed from one peril into another. Yet they were being moved to a higher level of society. It was difficult for Jon to imagine that the people of Lomooro would be cruel to him or his two companions if they were known to be from the Galactic Federation. He had tried to explain to Tanín one evening about his origin, but the man had found it impossible to even begin to understand. But surely there were scientists in the cities—men who would understand the meaning of his story. Nonetheless, Jon was not foolish enough to allow himself much more than a vague hope.

There were a lot of things on Lomooro of which he

knew nothing. In one brief conversation Tanín had mentioned "the games," but guards had ordered them back to work before Jon was able to question the man further. He had forgotten the matter until now. Something in the other man's eyes had suggested it was more than a harmless sport. The Lomoorians were a warlike people, bickering and battling between themselves in the belief that conflict and battle kept the soul clean. It had surely kept them actively involved in endless wars, from what Tanín had revealed of Lomoorian history. It had always been so, as far back as the memory of his people went. Such they were taught by the High Captain's Teachers.

By now all the Raiders had left the Rals' village and formed in a long line, awaiting the word to move. The prisoners were ordered to stand. Shortly the caravan filed slowly into the jungle along one of the well-marked trails leading from the village.

Jon asked over his shoulder: "How far is Nal-Iò?"

"Two, three marches."

One of the guards poked Jon with a spear. "Silence, slave."

During the long walk through the jungle, past half a dozen creeks and along a river, Jon found his mind spinning with endless questions. What kind of life would they lead in Nal-Iò? What were their chances of escape? And just exactly what were "the Games?"

At their noon rest for eating, Jon talked to Tanín. They were sitting along the bank of a broad river which Tanín called Boltor—the major waterway across the land.

"Our city lies south along the River Boltor, many marches." He pointed in the direction from which they had come.

"What can we expect in Nal-Iò, besides being sold into slavery?" Jon asked.

"Hard work, if you are not lucky in getting a good master. If you behave well and do not try to escape, you will live long. If not, it will be quick death, or to the Games." The man hesitated, studying Jon carefully. "Chances are that you—and I, come to think of it—will be trained for the Games. Professional Warrior-slaves. But if you are good at the battle, you will survive a long time. I have known warrior-slaves to last for many years and finally be given their freedom because they were so popular."

Jon needed no more information to understand. The Games were slaughters performed for the public who gloried in the battle and death of those taking part in the show.

Mari nudged him. "What are you talking about, Jon? What did he say? Where are we being taken?"

Jon was amazed at how little Mari really knew about their situation. He looked at her; a sense of guilt and pain stabbed at him. How could he have been so preoccupied that he ignored Mari? After a moment of thought, he was able to rationalize his action. She was safe; the future loomed dark and forbidding and it was only logical that he be concerned about it first.

Mari had changed since they were separated at the Rals' village. Her skin had taken on a deep tan. Her eyes strangely had not lost their innocent glow or their spark of hope. But some of the frightened, inexperienced child had disappeared. He was looking at a fully mature woman who had learned to accept what she knew of her fate and make the best of it. The change was startling. But the woman was still defenseless to survive alone in this hostile world.

Jon quickly told her what he had learned of Lomooro from Tanín; and something of the fate which was in store for them.

"Even though I plan on escaping at the first possible chance—if things do not work out well for us—I do think we should take every precaution we can."

She nodded silently.

He was about to tell her that it might be best to let all the Lomoorians believe that they were man and woman, when their attention was attracted by the shouting of male voices.

Two Raiders were coming their way: one was the leader of the band, Bal-jan-dà; the other was a young man with an ugly scar across his right cheek.

"I will pay whatever price you demand," the young man said.

"But where will you get the price?" Bal-jan-dà retorted.

"I will get it. Just let me have the woman."

The two men stopped opposite Jon and Mari.

"Let me have her," the young Raider pleaded, "and I will pay anything you ask."

Jon now recognized the man as one of the guards who had fastened the neck irons to the prisoners.

Bal-jan-dà looked down at Mari. After a moment's consideration, he said: "Lorn, why do you wish this strange woman as a slave?"

"Lorn-jan-dà would like to have her as his woman!" The man fingered his scar. "None of our tribe will take me!"

As Jon studied the man, he could easily understand why. Never had he seen such an ugly face. The scar ran along his right cheek and up into the eye, which was pale and milky.

Before the other men could say anything, Jon rose to his feet. "He can't have her."

Bal-jan-dà glared at Jon. "Why do you say so?" The Raider's voice was harsh, angry.

"She is mine!" Jon announced, placing an arm around Mari and silently praying she would understand.

Lorn-jan-dà drew his long knife and raised it above his head.

Bal-jan-dà grabbed his companion's wrist. "No!"

"If he is dead," Lorn-jan-dà snarled, hatred burning in his eyes, "she will no longer be his woman!"

"And we lose two slaves. You cannot have her. This settles the matter." Bal-jan-dà released the other's wrist. "That is the end of it."

But the look which Lorn-jan-dà shot at Jon as they turned to leave revealed that this was far from the end of the matter.

The rest of that day, Jon felt death breathing down his neck. Several times he saw Lorn-jan-dà staring hatefully at him. Tanín, who had watched the complete exchange, warned Jon. "He no more believes you are this woman's man than I. And he will kill you before we get to Nal-Iò, if he can. It will seem accidental. I know his type. He will do anything to have his way!"

"What do you mean? You don't believe me?"

Tanín grinned. "You do not act like she is your woman. Not the way I would act if she were mine. She is beautiful and I can imagine your wanting her. And I understand your reasons for claiming her as your own. You are to be admired for such bravery. But you might die for it. What is she truly to you?"

Before Jon could answer, the march was taken up and all conversation forcefully silenced.

That evening, camping inland some hours march from the River Boltor, Jon introduced Tanín to Mari and suggested that she begin learning the language of Lomooro. "It is simple enough," Jon said. "Not much different from our own."

Mari grinned. "I understand enough already. Picked it up at the village, around the cook fires. In fact, enough to thank you for saving me from a rather unpleasant fate." She shuddered. "I would rather die than become that... that thing's woman."

Jon studied Mari. He could not say exactly how he felt toward her. She came from a completely different society. Yet now they were both on the same social level: slaves.

That night and the next, Jon found it difficult to sleep. Tanín and Mari had been so friendly. There was no doubt that the man found Mari quite desirable. When sleep finally came, dreams of Mari tormented his rest.

Then finally came the last day of their march. That morning the Raiders prepared a warm brownish mush which tasted much like Earth-corn. Tanín told Jon that this mush was called *tons* and was made of the tone-grain which grew in this region.

The food which the Raiders had served before was a hard, dry, salty, smoked meat. Considering the nomadic life of the Raiders, the smoked meat was a logical choice as a daily food. Jon had learned that the Raiders actually lived in the desert regions of Lomooro—open plains which surrounded the lush jungles—where they left the women and children while on raids such as this.

Tanín explained about the mushy *tons* as they were eating. "They consider it something special, and only prepare it when they are about to enter one of the cities to do business. They believe that warm food is better on the stomach—and better for men who are about to enter into business matters. Otherwise they use the dried meat, which is prepared for them by the women."

Red asked: "The city of Nal-Iò is close, then?"

"Not far. Then the fun begins." Tanín's words held no humor. "Outside the city wall they will market us, body and soul, for goods, or *Tals*—which are pieces of metal with the mark of Nal-Iò on it. With the *Tals* they can get many things that cannot be brought to the city wall. Some of them will go to the market places—Bal-jan-dà and the Jan-dà Council. Here they will get food and clothing to take back to their plains and desert homes. Tonight, though, they will have a great feast."

Jon saw Lorn-jan-dà looking at him from some distance and was reminded of the man's threat. "So far I seem to have been saved from the revenge of Lorn-jan-dà."

"Let's hope it continues," Tanín offered. "He might try something between here and Nal-Iò. The city is on a cliff above the jungle. The trail is steep and zigzags up the cliffs. Watch out, for even in the city of Nal-Iò you may not be safe. Lorn-jan-dà is mad. I have seen many of his kind in the Raiders. They will kill just for the pleasure. In your case, he might kill you even after you are sold."

"That won't do him any good," Jon pointed out. "It wouldn't give him Mari!"

"He could steal her, or maybe buy her back from the owner. It does not matter. Possibly he will suggest to the master that you be killed; that way it will be possible for him to take possession of the beautiful woman slave. And Lorn-jan-dà would be willing to kill his own mother for the right price. You have made a dangerous enemy. And there is no legal defense if you were to kill him in protecting yourself."

The four of them talked at some length while the Raiders were breaking camp. But when Jon brought up the subject of escape, Tanín shook his head.

"It is quite impossible. It has never been done before."

"If it has never been done, what is to say it cannot be done? At least a man should try. Has it been tried?"

"Yes—but you always end up in the Games, with no chance of surviving. That is sure death, for the Games under those circumstances mean death at the jaws of some jungle beast." He was silent for a moment. "But it is a good dream—for woman and children to believe in. A man must be realistic."

The Lomoorian was silent for a moment, then said: "You see, my friend, once inside the city wall there is little hope of escape. They will have guards with bows and arrows stationed along the wall at all times of day and night. The chances of getting outside the wall are very slim. Surviving in the jungle alone just cannot be done. If you got as far as the jungle, who knows, maybe by some act of the gods you might survive. But..." He shrugged.

Jon was about to explain about the explosive pellets when the guards ordered them to stand. The march during the next few hours was far slower than before, with many more stops along the way. It seemed as if they were purposely taking their time.

Then suddenly they came out of the narrow trail and into a large clearing which faced huge, naked cliffs rising some three thousand feet toward the deep, blue-green sky of Lomooro. Jon could see the bare expanse of an aged wall beyond which showed pointed towers. It was his first view of Nal-Iò—the city where they would all be sold into slavery— where he might die.

Reality now overwhelmed him as he looked at those sheer, jagged, reddish-brown cliffs and up to the walled city with its needle towers.

If it were not for Mari, Jon realized, he could have been tempted to take the easy way out. Fight, right then and there. Be killed, but kill as many of the Raiders as possible. Or, conceivably, escape. But what faced him after that?

Then the column of mounted Raiders started forward, heading toward the base of the cliff at a point where a startlingly narrow trail moved back and forth up to the summit and finally to the walled city.

Jon felt himself jabbed with a spear point. He turned angrily and found Lorn-jan-dà standing behind him. The man's scar slashed an evil smile into something horrible to behold. His dead eye gazed blindly at Jon; the good one squinted.

"There is yet time," Lorn-jan-dà announced, prodding

Jon once more with the spear and this time drawing blood. "I think you will become very violent. A shame. Those cliffs. A long fall!" Cackling laughter followed.

Jon looked up the face of the cliff and shuddered. A slip—or an excuse to use the spear—might end his life. The neck collar would merely hang Jon and break his neck if he happened to slip from the ledge too fast. While the collar was not large or heavy, it now became uncomfortably tight.

Lorn-jan-dà shoved him and grunted something under his breath. "Hurry!" Lorn-jan-dà ordered, nicking Jon once more with the spear as they came to the beginning of the pathway winding up the hill. "Hurry. We don't have all day."

Slowly the caravan moved up the side of the cliff. Jon thought only about the fact that living must be better, under any conditions, than death. It was the only thing which kept his temper under control. The temptation to turn and rip the spear out of the man's hands was almost uncontrollable. It would not be too difficult. But even if he managed to kill the Raider, others would kill him. Lorn-jan-dà was not worth it.

The hot sun burned down upon them. Jon's body was covered with a mixture of sweat and blood. It seemed they would never rest. Jon looked at Mari and saw her stumble. He quickly grabbed her arm to steady her.

"Thanks."

Jon nodded. "We have to rest some time." He looked at Lorn-jan-dà, but there was no pity in the man's narrowed good eye. A short time later, however, the caravan came to a halt.

"Tired?" Jon looked at Mari, who was leaning her head against the cliff. He spoke in the Galactic Federation modern language.

"I guess I have to get used to it," she said weakly.

"We'll escape somehow, then go to Tal-Jaÿ with Tanín." He looked deep into Mari's eyes, trying to drill this hope home. "The main thing is to keep alive! Do you understand?"

For a moment she did not move; then she nodded.

"Time is on our side. Remember that. Believe it. And don't give up hope. We have the explosive atomatic pellets. They will make escape possible—at the right moment."

She stared at him. "Do you really believe it?" There was a pleading light in her eyes which seemed to beg him to believe it himself, and convince her that it was true.

"Of course I do. Otherwise I'd say to kill yourself. Life as slaves is no life at all. Without hope, we have nothing. But a few days, weeks, months—even years—is not the end. We will get out of this, in time. And don't forget, Tanín will see to it that we are welcomed as friends in Tal-Jaÿ. That is what we must look forward to. Tal-Jaÿ. Then we'll search for other survivors from the space liner."

He grabbed Mari's shoulder, squeezing the soft flesh in his intensity. Suddenly it was the most important thing in the world to give her hope.

"We have life and we have time! Escape is possible! Freedom!" He fairly shouted the words at her.

She winced from the pressure of his hands. "I believe you, Jon. I believe that Jon Handon can make escape possible! But, in the meantime... we will have to get used to it. Being slaves..

The guards came then and ordered them to their feet.

Jon spoke to Mari in their own language. "Don't forget the atomatic pellets." But he knew that there was only one escape for them: Tal-Jaÿ, Tanín's home, where they would be met as friends. But this lay in the opposite direction from that taken by the other scout-boat before its disappearance. Then Jon realized how hopeless it might be to search for the other survivors. Their fate might easily have been capture or death. The jungle was a deadly trap. On their march, burning eyes had watched from the brush. Tanín had explained that the jungle was filled with savage, man-eating beasts. Besides the Lombor—the name Tanín gave the beast which Red and Jon had killed on their first day on the planet—two other giants of the jungle were highly dangerous. The Lient was all claws—eight-footed and twice as large as a man. The Palt, larger than the Lombor, had a long neck and tail, either of which could be quite deadly. It was the most feared of the jungle beasts because they came in packs. They were far safer in the city of Nal-Iò as slaves than free to wander the jungle perils.

Jon's body ached with a dozen cuts from Lorn-jan-dà

spear.

The ledge along which they had been marching widened to some eight feet. Then suddenly, when they were about twenty feet from the top of the cliff, the Raider went crazy with rage, screaming at the top of his voice. He leaped at Jon and struck out with his spear, hitting his prisoner on the back of the head.

Through the blaze of pain, Jon heard the man bellowing: "I'll kill you for that! Kill you!"

He felt the impact of the spear's butt in his stomach, then Jon's reflexes took over. Automatically his right arm shot out, hand stiff, fingers held together and straight. His fingers cut deep into the man's throat. His second rapid blow was a left fist to the stomach.

Lorn-jan-dà dropped his spear, gasping for breath. He was half unconscious from pain by now, gasping like some dying beast.

Jon pulled his right arm back and was about to slash downward with a murderous blow at the other's neck when his sanity abruptly returned and he realized what had happened. He heard a yell from one of the mounted Raiders on the trail below, and knew that his fate was automatically sealed. Death could be the only result of what he had done to the Raider, Lorn-jan-dà.

THE SLAVES OF LOMOORO, BY CHARLES NUETZEL

CHAPTER SIX

Londì

Standing over the agonized Lorn-jan-dà, Jon was sure that immediate death would follow. He turned and looked at Mari, whose frightened eyes were filled with tears.

Then Jon saw Tanín's grinning face. "He deserved to die!" Tanín announced. "But you did right to stop."

"That's not going to help me," Jon pointed out bitterly.

"Maybe. Bal-jan-dà is an honorable man. If I tell him the truth, he will take my word as a Tal-Jaÿ Warrior Lord. And I will tell him immediately!"

Jon saw Raiders coming toward him from both sides, bows drawn to the full extent of their long, metal-tipped arrows. "I'm afraid it might come a little late," Jon observed.

Tanín quickly raised his hand high in the air, attracting instant attention. "I am Tanín, Warrior Lord of the Tal-Jaÿs, and I demand to have words with Bal-jan-dà! This man had no choice but to defend himself."

As Tanín spoke, the Raiders came to a halt only a few feet away. For a moment they stared at him blankly, unmoving, as if they could not quite believe that a slave-prisoner would speak in such a manner. Then Lorn-jan-dà, lying on the ground and clutching his throat, screamed at the top of his voice. "Kill them both!"

"Bal-jan-dà will not be happy if two slaves are killed," Tanín announced. "Let Bal-jan-dà decide! He is a just and fair man. We will take his decision once he has heard our story."

As Tanín spoke, Jon picked up the spear. In one swift movement, before anybody could realize what he was up to, he thrust the point at Lorn-jan-dà's throat. "Do as he says," Jon shouted, "or this man dies!"

The warriors hesitated, murmuring unsurely. Tanín quickly added, "This man could easily have killed Lorn-jan-dà before—as you can see now. And he can still do so."

"Go get Bal-jan-dà!" one of the Raiders demanded of the man beside him. "We will watch."

It was some time before the caravan had been alerted to a halt, and Bal-jan-dà was in a terrible temper when he finally came storming up, his shining robes slashing angrily around his legs. He looked at Jon, who was still holding the spear at Lorn-jan-dà's throat. "What's the meaning of this?" he bellowed.

Jon dropped the spear. Its purpose had been served. The Raider Chief had arrived.

Lorn-jan-dà had recovered somewhat and now quickly stood. Before he could speak, Tanín stepped forward.

"I am Tanín, Warrior Lord of Tal-Jaÿ. You will remember having seen me at my father's home last year." Bal-jan-dà nodded angrily and Tanín continued. "This guard was attempting to kill Jon Handon. He had been prodding him all the way up the trail with his spear—for no other reason than that he is the man of this woman Lorn-jan-dà desires!" Tanín spat on the ground to make his contempt more clear.

Bal-jan-dà glared at his subject, then the anger in his eyes focused on Lorn-jan-dà. "You will not share in the profits!" the Raider leader announced. "Keep him away from the prisoners."

Under his breath, Lorn-jan-dà said, "You die!" His remark was directed at both of them, but could not be heard beyond a few feet.

The rest of the march was silent. Once they reached the top and saw the huge walls of Nal-Iò close at hand, Jon gasped his surprise. "I would not have guessed it was so large."

The walls rose some twenty feet above them. At the top stood guards, stationed at posts some twenty feet apart. The walls were reddish brown; in places their surface had crumbled with age, revealing large, stone blocks.

Jon realized that the people who had landed on the planet must have done so many centuries before. Yet there had been no record of the fact in the star charts. Some companies, he knew, made it a habit to merely observe from orbit, send a claimer-rocket down onto one of the continents, and thus legally take possession of the planet in the age-old manner.

Lomooro was far off the normal star routes, and it was the only world in its system on which humans could live and survive easily. This explained why no Galactic colony had been formed. Apparently the original company had planned on turning it into some tourist resort. Plans abandoned, the planet had slipped into a dusty, aging company file and been forgotten. This was not uncommon. It was also not uncommon for the company to change hands, or simply cease to exist. And this was the case with Lomooro. There was no doubt in Jon's mind that this planet had held human life on its surface for at least a thousand years.

The caravan finally came to a stop just outside a huge arched metal gate which was now slowly opening.

"Get seated!" said one of their guards, eyeing Jon and Tanín in an amused manner. It seemed almost as if the man liked what had gone on a short time before. It was not hard to imagine that Lorn-jan-dà was not popular among his fellow Raiders.

As soon as the Raiders had set up a quick camp of large, colorful tents, tied their mounts in a circle and placed a watch of some ten men on them and their prisoners, they went into the city.

Jon looked beyond the gates and saw a street evenly lined with high, tower-topped buildings. People swarmed out of the city to the Raiders who were guarding the prisoners. Friendly conversation seemed to pass between Raiders and the Citizens of Nal-Iò.

Jon examined the dress of the city folk. They were Commoners, according to Tanín, who tended shops, worked as laborers at certain times during the year, and served the Nobles and Rich of the city. Both men and women were dressed in simple but colorful clothing made of two pieces. The tops hung over their shoulders, circling around the neck in a snug manner and hanging loose to the hips. For the men, form-fitting slacks hugged around their legs. For the women, open skirts dropped down in flowing folds around their ankles.

To Jon's surprise, most of the people were quite handsome.

Some time later the chief of the Jan-dà tribe and his fellows returned from the city, followed by richly dressed men. These, Tanín pointed out, were the Nobles and Lords of the city. Each rode upon heavy-jeweled chairs borne by four half-naked slaves.

These men were dressed in long, shiny, one-piece robes and had strands of jeweled necklaces falling from around their necks down to the belts which supported long, slender-sheathed swords. Their slaves were dressed in leather harnesses that crisscrossed the chest and back, and a g-string about their middles. Oddly enough, some of the slaves were armed with swords and knives.

Jon asked Tanín about this, and the man shrugged, "What can a lone slave do against a whole city? Armed or unarmed, makes no difference. Or be recaptured. As a slave becomes more trusted, he is given more responsibilities, and finally armed. There is little fear that he will attempt violence or escape. You are obsessed by this idea of escaping. Forget it, for it will give you only death."

Bal-jan-dà spent his time with the Nobles and Lords, talking in a glorious manner about the wonderful slaves which the Jan-dàs had brought the people of Nal-Iò.

Tanín explained. "He goes through this kind of show, which means little to anyone. These rich Lords will pick those of us they desire, offer a price. Bal-jan-dà will argue, attempt to get more, then finally the sale will be completed at a price worthy of our hides! The remainder will be offered to the Commoners for what little trade can be squeezed out of them. To be sold to a Commoner is a far more terrible fate, for they have little refinement, only wanting someone to beat and push around. A Lord will make life far easier. There is always a chance that you might be trained for the Games—

which could mean a quick end. Though from what I saw in that moment of action against Lorn-jan-dà a short time ago, I would say your ability as a fighting man might make you a hero of the Games in short order. You have the build, and the speed with your hands was remarkable. I have never seen such an attack."

Tanín shrugged. "In my case, it does not matter much. For life is life. We breathe, we eat, and we live. We survive one way or another! You are a wise man, having claimed the woman as your mate. There is a chance of gaining the house of a Lord. This will make life far easier. I might be sold to the Palace—or the Games Lord. The latter would..." Again he shrugged. "It really does not matter."

Jon was about to ask how they might meet again, but Bal-jan-dà came up opposite them leading half a dozen finely dressed Lords who kept their eyes greedily flowing over the chained prisoners.

One man in particular seemed to find Mari extremely fascinating. He was heavy, big-eyed, and had the appearance of a bully. He could not be much older than Jon himself, but there was that about the eyes which suggested a primitive violence bordering on insanity. He silently listened to Bal-jan-dà's introduction concerning Mari.

"And here, my Lords, is a fine, and outstanding example of womanhood, a great addition to your wife's maids, for with her comes this tall, broad-shouldered warrior, who is dressed—much as she—in strange and alien clothing as if he had come from another world."

This brought on a burst of laughter from the people around them. One voice called out: "From what world would he come? The heavens above, like our First High Captain? Or the world below? For there is none other than Lomooro!" More laughter bellowed.

The Raider chief shrugged, waiting until the laughter had stopped. "No matter where he comes from, what strange and distant city, he all but killed one of my armed sub chiefs! He would make a magnificent addition to the armed guard of some Lord. Or a great warrior for the Games, winning many Tals for his master in game bets."

A fat, evil-looking Lord blurted out: "How much for the

woman...and her friend?" This last was as if an after-statement, spat out with great distaste.

"Two thousand Tals, five young Martos stallions, and the finest gowns to clothe my warriors," Bal-jan-dà announced.

Tanín nudged Jon's arm. "He is about to rob the fool!"

Having no idea of what value the people of Lomooro might place on either slaves they bought or the products which they paid for them, Jon could only guess what value Bal-jan-dà had placed on himself and Mari. But, guessing the kind of dealer the old Raider obviously was, and judging from the reactions of the others around them, it was not hard to conclude that Bal-jan-dà had demanded an outlandish price.

The fat man gulped; his face grew red. "You attempt to rob Balt-Lot!"

"Take it or leave it!" Bal-jan-dà retorted, standing with fists on his hips, face expressionless, jaw thrust stubbornly out.

For some moments the man who called himself Balt-Lot gazed yearningly at Mari. Then he finally grunted: "Half that amount and that's all you get!"

"This great warrior will make twenty times the price if you but train him for the Games!" Bal-jan-dà spat.

"I take your word for that. Not a Tal more." The fat man's eyes were gleaming with hot excitement as he stared at Mari.

"But the warrior!" Bal-jan-dà cried.

Balt-Lot glared at Jon; the evil expression in his deep-set small eyes told all too clearly the fate he had in store for this male prisoner-slave.

"Are there no others who want them?" Bal-jan-dà inquired, making a sweep of the other Lords and Nobles surrounding him. His voice was high, almost desperate. But when there was no response, he merely shrugged. "So it must be. You rob me! You rob my tribe. You insult my people. But it must be!"

"You rob Lord Balt-Lot. No doubt you stole the slaves from some Ral's village! But I'll get my worth from them. Both of them!" Lord Balt-Lot threw an angry glance at the

Raider and then returned his gaze to Mari. "Free them, and I will leave. You may come to my house and collect your price. As these Lords are my witness!"

As Mari was being freed from the neck ring, Jon chanced a quick plea to Red in their own language. "Keep the explosives if at all possible. We may need them later."

The other man nodded, then blurted out: "Take care of her!"

"Quiet!" one of the guards warned, pressing a spear to Red's chest. "Quiet!"

Then with a jerk of the spear, the man ordered Jon and Mari toward their new owner, Lord Balt-Lot, who was now grinning from ear to ear.

Escape was impossible; they were surrounded by dozens of Raiders, and the people of Nal-Iò. The minute the Raider guard had turned them over to Lord Balt-Lot, the fat man assigned one of his own men to watch over them, then returned to his jewel-encrusted golden chair, carved with a design of flowers and vines interwoven into beautiful patterns.

The man who had been assigned to keep an eye on Jon and Mari was a huge brute, armed with a long sword which hung in the simple leather sheath at his waist. He was clean shaven, much as the other people of Nal-Iò, but like the slaves was naked to the waist. The muscles of his back and shoulders were huge, rippling; his movement that of a jungle cat. But the face was mobile, and as they followed Lord Balt-Lot, the man smiled pleasantly. "I would be careful, for Lord Balt-Lot has you marked. But even he cannot go against custom. A fair warning, friend. For surely I would rather have you as a friend than otherwise."

Jon looked at the tall man more carefully, surprised by his friendly voice and manner. He had a large nose and thick lips, but the man's brown eyes were amazingly gentle. Here was a man who could easily become a friend, and Jon needed as many as he could get on this world. Obviously he was some kind of favored slave.

"What do you think he has planned for me?" Jon asked.

"The Games, possibly. A quick death—if he can arrange it." The man studied Jon. "For your sake, I only hope that

Raider was speaking the truth about your ability to fight. It would not surprise me if Lord Balt-Lot had some entertainment in mind. This would not be the first time he arranged a feast under such circumstances. Of all the Lords in Nal-Iò, he is the only one who would be so low as to take great pleasure in having your woman, after ridding himself of you."

Jon sighed, following their new master who was now being carried toward the walled city by four bare-backed slaves.

Jon asked: "Are you one of the..."

"Slaves?" The other grinned. "Yes, I am known as Londì, Slave-warrior for Lord Balt-Lot. Master-at-Arms, and his Champion! And pray to the gods that Lord Balt-Lot does not have a party planned for you this evening, for it will be I who will have to kill you." Londì said this last so casually that Jon could not for a moment grasp the full meaning of his words.

"I would have to fight you?" he asked, open amazement in his voice.

"And die. For it would be to the death, and I am known as one of the best warriors in Nal-Iò!" This was said as a mere statement of fact.

"But you are a slave."

"Yes," the other admitted simply.

"Aren't they afraid you might turn on his Lordship, or return to your people? Escape to freedom?"

"Where would I be treated better?" Londì asked. "Freedom is a strange word. It has many meanings. What kind of freedom? To wander through the jungles and be killed? To go back to my home, Fan-jèk, as a Commoner? To stay here? Here at least I have all that a man might expect. Though Lord Balt-Lot is a harsh master, he is no more cruel than many others—or the world which surrounds us. I have become his Champion, and in that position I have all the food and wine I want, and plenty of slave girls!" Londì shrugged. "What would escape mean to me? Returning to Fan-jèk to work hard at my father's food stall, or become a soldier, or bodyguard for some Lord."

"But are you not afraid of being killed someday in a

68

fight?"

"We all die in time," Londì said matter-of-factly. "One time might be as good as another, as long as we have lived our life to the fullest. I am best at fighting. I am what they call a professional. If I fight here, or someplace else, it really does not matter, does it? It is easier here. Plenty of women, and living in a rich man's house. No, I can see no reason to escape. I have been here for too long. Nobody escapes, anyway, so such talk is foolish."

In silence they walked through the huge double gates of the city of Nal-Iò.

Mari had been hanging close to Jon like a frightened little girl. "How like the primitive cities of which the history books of Earth tell and show us," she said. "Or the cities of Mallo or Tempests."

Jon knew little about the history of the human race and less of the history of Earth from which Mankind had seeded, gone through its early childhood and reached out toward the stars and maturity. But still he found himself strongly impressed by what he now saw.

The buildings were two to three stories high. The arched doors and windows had lacy designs in bold relief running along their borders. Each building had at least one balcony, upon which colorful flowers grew. From some of the windows and on many of the balconies, people observed the street through which Jon and the others were now passing, but paid little attention to them.

The streets were quite busy with heavy traffic: merchants shouting each other down, trying to sell their products of pottery, food and clothing from the doorways; people who were shopping on foot or riding through on Lomoorian mounts. The movement of this traffic had no apparent order; the street had neither sidewalks nor any kind of divider as in modern civilized cities of the Federation. Here they intermingled, going in every possible direction.

Londì kept a close watch upon the two newly acquired slaves. Even though his words and attitude had been friendly, Jon fully realized that the man would have killed either one of them without warning if they attempted to escape. Yet it was a casual guarding, since the man hardly expected anyone to try an escape.

Jon was puzzled by Londì's reasoning. Obviously a slave, the man was not interested in changing his status in any way. Yet Londì was not much different in his attitude toward captivity than Tanín had seemed to be. This very lack of interest in changing the status quo could work to Jon's benefit, he realized.

The group, which was now holding fairly close together, turned down a side street and almost immediately came to a halt in front of an impressive building which stood separated from the others by an expansive wall some ten feet high circling it from both sides of the front entrance.

The face of the building was trimmed in a glittering reddish stone that had been delicately cut in beautiful patterns to form human figures and twisting vines, locking together and blending into a pattern of more faces and bodies.

Just before they started to enter the building, Lord Balt-Lot called out to Londì. "Bring the slaves to the living room. I will look them over more carefully now that we are alone."

Mari seemed to drift a little closer to Jon as they were ushered into the building and down a remarkably plain green hallway. They were immediately taken into a sparsely furnished room.

A long, low, backless sofa was placed in the middle of the room in front of a stone fireplace. Over the fireplace hung two beautifully jeweled long, slender swords crossed over a rather bulky shield of glossy brass-colored metal. A couple of wood and leather chairs were placed a few feet from the sofa, at each end, facing one another.

Outside of Mari, Londì and Jon, the room was totally empty.

"We will wait here until the Master comes!" Londì announced. He was studying Jon and Mari very closely now. Suddenly he asked: "What manner of strange clothing do you wear?"

Jon grinned. "If I told you we came from another world, would you believe me?"

"Of course you come from another city, a strange one, possibly far away, for your clothing is of a different design

70

from that of Nal-Iò or other nearby cities."

"No, from another planet. Like this world, but a different planet." Jon felt frustrated. There was simply no way of explaining to the Lomoorian what he was talking about.

Londì shook his head. "Whatever...well, your clothing is strange."

Just then Lord Balt-Lot entered from a side door, followed by three tough looking men, each armed with a sword and knife, and a small hand club which was strapped to the right wrist. These men were dressed in leather pants and shirts which were pulled tightly around them, giving the appearance of armored uniforms. The three brutes looked quite capable of enjoyment in using their clubs on any person foolish enough to argue with them. These, Jon would learn later, were Lord Balt-Lot's personal guards, hired from the Commoners of the city.

Lord Balt-Lot stepped up to Jon and Mari, stopping a couple of feet in front of them.

"Well!" He grinned triumphantly, like a man who has captured a giant prize and is very pleased with himself. For a moment his eyes turned to Mari, fairly caressing her face and figure. Then he turned his attention to Jon. "You are a tough one, is that right?" He reached out and pinched Jon's right arm, just above the elbow. "Strong enough. Let me see your teeth!"

Jon stood there for a moment, stunned. The man was treating him like some prize animal.

"Your teeth !" Lord Balt-Lot fairly shouted.

When Jon still hesitated, one of the leather-clad brutes grabbed him by the arm, from behind. It was a mistake which the man quickly realized, for Jon responded automatically, angrily. If there had been time to think unemotionally, Jon might not have attacked.

From the moment the reflex action took place, moving his muscles, Jon was detached, yet aware of everything he did. It was too late to stop the attack, and very much like an enjoyable dream. It was almost as if he wanted to show them just what kind of person he really was—right from the beginning, regardless of what it might cost. He was like a

71

drunken man. It was an insane risk, already in action before he could stop it.

He grabbed the startled Nal-Iò bodyguard, twisted around, still holding the other's right arm. As the fellow yelled in surprise and pain, Jon shot out two quick jabs with his left hand into the other's neck. The brute gasped. His eyes bulged, then he slumped slowly to the floor, unconscious.

The other two guards started toward Jon. Lord Balt-Lot shouted: "Wait!"

For a moment nobody moved, then Lord Balt-Lot slowly grinned. An oily, evil expression contorted his features. "You are a spirited one. Well, there are ways of taking care of you. But all in good time. In good time."

Then Lord Balt-Lot turned and faced Mari. He quickly reached out and touched her arms and shoulder. She cringed away from the contact.

"What's wrong, child?" Lord Balt-Lot sneered.

Before Mari could answer, Jon blurted: "She's mine. So keep your hands off her!"

Lord Balt-Lot glared at Jon. "Now you've gone far enough," he spat. "Nobody tells me what to do, not even the High Captain! And surely no slave! I could have you killed for that."

The man clapped his hands together and suddenly the two men in leather drew their swords, which gleamed in the light as they flashed toward Jon's body.

For a moment Jon was certain that he was about to die. His body coiled like a spring, every muscle tensed, alert, his arms slightly forward, his legs bent. Yet even as he prepared to defend himself, Jon realized it would be quite useless. Before two naked razor-sharp blades, he was helpless.

Then Lord Balt-Lot flung his right arm into the air. "Wait!" he shouted. "I have better plans for this loud-mouthed slave."

For a moment he was silent, then he said:

"After all, I have paid a good price for the two of them. And it is a simple matter to kill this man! Some sport might be a little more interesting. How would you like a little sport, man?" The last remark was a demanding one, not really a question. "Londì here is a giant among fighters. Nobody has yet beaten him. He has killed with his bare hands some hundred men in the Arena, twenty men in this very house. I think it is about time that he killed his twenty-first."

Lord Balt-Lot laughed, but it was the laughter of insanity.

The others in the room were stony, silent.

"Don't count me dead yet!" Jon snapped.

Lord Balt-Lot laughed even harder at that. The huge rolls of fat on his chest and stomach vibrated; sounds burst from his mouth, bounding around the room like the ugly explosive grating of a zethena. It was some time before he was able to control the laughter. Then he glared at Jon. "You will die wonderfully, and we will drink to your slow and painful death. We will laugh and drink as you scream in agony."

With that, Lord Balt-Lot turned and moved to the door through which he had entered. "Take him to the slaves' quarters. Take the girl to my women's wing."

Then he disappeared, slamming the door behind him.

THE SLAVES OF LOMOORO, BY CHARLES NUETZEL

CHAPTER SEVEN

In the House of Balt-Lot

For a moment nobody spoke, then Londì broke the silence. "I am truly sorry."

He turned to the other two men, who were holding their swords within a few inches of Jon. "Do as Master Lord Balt-Lot has ordered."

The two men prodded Jon gently with the swords. Without a word Jon went down the hallway, moving between the two escort guards to the back of the large house, past several doors which led to various big rooms.

The smell of cooking food filtered through the air just before they went out through a small door, leaving the main house. They stepped into an enclosed backyard which was beautifully gardened with creeping vines along walls sprinkled with a multitude of colorful flowers.

The two guards pushed Jon toward a large building on the opposite side of the yard. This building was a simple structure, with a dozen doors cut in its face.

"In there," one of the guards ordered, shoving the captive in front of a narrow door.

Jon pushed the door open and looked inside. The room was quite small, having a bunk and a wooden stool. There was only enough space left to stand while changing clothes.

"These are your quarters for the day," one of the guards grinned, sheathing his sword. "But once Londì takes care of you, you will be meat for the Game Lients. Master Lord Balt-Lot will not get his full price for you—but I imagine the entertainment will be worth the cost!"

The two guards laughed, shoved him inside the room, and slammed the door shut. Jon heard the sound of a bolt sliding into place. He was a prisoner.

He sat on the hard cot-like bed which was pushed up against the wall. Then finally he stretched out, trying to relax his muscles. He had learned in the Space Service that it was important to get a good rest before entering battle. That he must fight for his life within a few hours was a certainty.

* * * * * * *

Mari had been taken to a tiny room containing two stools. Two doorways faced each other—one through which she had entered, and another which remained closed. Feminine voices chattered liltingly from behind this latter door. But her ears were not tuned to conversation. All thoughts were centered on Jon Handon.

She sat facing the closed door. The stool was nothing but a framework of wood supporting tightly stretched leather.

A choking dread overcame Mari as she realized that Jon would soon be dead and that there was nothing either of them could do about it. She buried her face in trembling hands. What was to become of her? The man who called himself Lord Balt-Lot would surely want to make her a plaything for his passions. The very thought sent a shiver through her.

Then she remembered the tremor she had experienced on first seeing Jon Handon, their first night on the space liner, in the dining room. He was obviously nursing a hangover at the time, and his uniform was wrinkled. When he sat next to her, Mari had fought an inner feeling which she could not understand, for she had never experienced it before. Jon Handon, Spaceman, professional killer, had spoken. And at the sound of his voice, the very inner linings of her nerves had reacted.

Now, sitting in the small room in the House of Balt-Lot, in Nal-Iò, on the planet Lomooro, Mari realized that the feeling had not been revulsion, as she had believed, but something completely different. It was not at all the same as what she was now experiencing at the thought of being used by the Master of this house.

Mari's head shook sadly from side to side, remembering all those days in the small scout-boat. She had kept aloof from the two men. How childish it all seemed now. How much of a change had taken place. Since those long nights alone in the Ral village, frightened and unable to escape any fate which might befall her, this change had solidified. Then the march to Nal-Iò under the guard of Lomoorian Raiders and, finally, being sold as a slave to Lord Balt-Lot. Mari felt it was the last ounce of humiliation she could take.

Sudden tears streamed down her cheeks. Mari wanted to run and never look back. But there was no running, no chance to escape without Jon Handon. No safe place to go on all this planet.

Mari realized now how much she had been depending on the man—a man she had believed she hated. She had used belief in his ability to protect her in some supernatural way as a form of self strength. But now, faced with the fact that Jon Handon was as helpless as any other human being, as helpless as herself, Mari felt complete defeat.

And terror.

When the door opened into the inner room a few moments later, Mari was sitting against the wall, glassy-eyed, pale, hands fallen lifelessly to her lap.

"Come, woman!" a harsh female voice ordered. "You begin your duties as chambermaid for Lady Balt-Lot."

Mari did not respond. The tall, hard-faced woman, dressed in a lacy yellow gown which showed off more of her beefy figure than it hid, jerked forward. She cruelly grabbed the almost unconscious girl.

Mari gasped; her eyes focused on the angular features for the first time. The face was framed with reddish hair which fell in long curls around broad, powerful shoulders. The lips were too pouty, too wide, the nose hooked, the eyes large and deep-set, hot with mocking anger.

"When Penty commands, you jump!" Without warning the woman struck Mari brutally across the face. "Come. I'll show you a little manners!"

Again the heavy hand slapped across Mari's face; for the first time in her life she felt fury eat its way into a burning, violent hatred. Mari's muscles coiled upon one another. She struck out a clawed hand, but she scratched through empty air. Something slammed her against the wall. Open-handed slaps hit back and forth across her face.

A moment later the woman named Penty threw Mari onto the floor of the inner room.

"You ever do anything like that again and you'll wish you'd never lived!" she screamed.

Mari got a quick impression of other women crowding around the two of them, but that was all she saw. Gasping, tears coursing down her cheeks, Mari struggled to her feet. Her only thought was a desire to commit murder. Before she could move a muscle, Penty leaped forward and kicked out a long, muscular leg. The woman's hard, pointed shoe made contact at the side of Mari's head.

The next thing she knew, the new female slave of Lord and Lady Balt-Lot was lying on a cot in a room plunged in total darkness.

* * * * * * *

Sleep had not come easily for Jon. He lay in the room wondering what had happened to Red and Tanín. But mostly he thought of Mari. If he were killed this evening—a possibility which he could not completely ignore—the woman's fate was assured. Death might be better for a girl such as Mari.

Hundreds of times in the past Jon had faced battle and the idea of dying, yet death had never seemed so real as it did now. A man went out and fought, killed the enemy, using every ounce of knowledge in his well-trained mind and body to keep alive. Jon had been a good soldier, a top professional, well versed in the modern techniques of Planetary Warfare. He knew atomatic guns of all types; he could kill a man with his hands, quickly and easily. He was an expert in hand-to-hand combat, using club, rifle butt, knife or bare fists. But he knew nothing of sword-play or the primitive weapons which the professional fighters of

Lomooro such as Londì might be able to put into use. He did not know the customs of this planet or what might happen if he managed to kill Londì.

Jon was mulling these facts over and over in his mind when the door suddenly burst open and Londì stepped in, closing the door behind him.

The tall man stood over Jon's bunk; from that angle he took on the proportions of some weird giant. But with all his mass and bulk, his eyes still held that vague suggestion of regret and distant friendship which Jon had noticed before.

Finally the man spoke. "May I sit?"

"I don't think it would be possible to stop you even if I so desired," he told Londì.

Londì sat; suddenly he seemed nothing more than a tall, sad-faced man.

"I am sorry," Londì began in a regretful voice, "that things turned out this way. I believe you would have made a good man-at-arms. We would have been friends." He shrugged, then looked at his large hands lying in his lap. "I will make it as painless as possible."

Jon looked at Londì with a sense of bewilderment. He tried to think of something to say, but words would not come.

"You handle yourself well with your hands. That's a trick I have never seen used by a man before. If you were to be given a chance to fight me in that manner, it is very possible that you might win. I would not know how to defend myself against such a strange attack."

"Then what will it be? Swords?"

Londì grinned. "More than that. Swords, knives, whip, battle axes, spears, mace—a bloody little assortment of death. One of each for both of us."

"Surely we can't use them all at once!" Jon exclaimed, puzzled that Londì was talking to him in this frank and friendly manner.

"We use what we want—when we want it. As simple as that." Londì shrugged again. It was the helpless gesture of one who can do nothing to change his own fate and is unhappy about it. "I wish I could kill you immediately. But Lord Balt-Lot will want a good, bloody show. I will have to cut you to pieces, carve the image of death on your body—a little cut here, a little pain there, until finally it will be necessary to kill you. Then death will seem a wonderful haven, escape from horrible pain. But I will make it as painless as possible, if you but help. Put on a good show. Every time I strike you, act as if you are in great pain. Make it look good and it will not be necessary to hurt you too much. It will be up to you."

Londì looked seriously at him for a moment, and it seemed to Jon that he could read the other's thoughts. Jon felt an instinctive liking for Londì, for the man was a professional soldier. An automatic respect had already started between them; given time, the bond might have been very strong.

"No, Londì. I will fight the best I can," Jon finally said, now feeling much the same as Londì. It was not going to be pleasant killing a man you did not hate, just for the excitement of some fat, degenerate weakling. It was different when facing an enemy. Yet, if Jon was able, he would defend himself, and in doing this would have to hurt and kill this gentle man sitting beside him. The weapons to be used were designed to inflict bloody and painful death.

Londì winced at Jon's words. "I'm truly sorry to hear that."

"I don't plan on dying, Londì," Jon finally managed.

"But you will, nonetheless." Londì stood, moved to the door, then turned to face Jon Handon. "And you will die in great pain, because that is the way of Lomooro, the way of Nal-Iò and the way of Lord Balt-Lot. That is life and... we cannot escape fate."

He started to turn, but Jon stopped him. "Then why not escape? Why not refuse to fight?"

Londì shook his head. "I told you before—there is nothing better for a man like myself. Food, wine and women. This or some kind of hell which is far more terrible than the one I am now forced to live."

"What will happen to Mari?" Jon asked the question even while fearing the answer. "The woman who came with me."

"She will be taken to Lord Balt-Lot's quarters. Probably

this evening, after you have been killed and fed to the Lients! If you wish, I will see to it that she is quietly and secretly killed in the night—when Lord Balt-Lot is asleep—as if she had killed herself."

The idea stunned Jon at first. The man had said it as if offering a great favor and service. But after a moment Jon realized that possibly it would be the only decent thing for Mari. Life here, with Lord Balt-Lot taking her to his rooms at night, would be a living hell. Death might be far better. He also realized the great personal danger Londi would expose himself to in performing such a deed.

"No," Jon finally said in a soft voice. "It is not for me to decide. But you might slip her a knife if I am killed. Let her have the chance to decide for herself."

Londi nodded understandingly. "As you desire. I do wish there were more I could do for you..."

Then the man opened the door and was gone. Jon sat there puzzled by the other's bold offer of friendship. It hardly made sense, unless it was a way for Londi to escape his personal guilt.

Hours later, the door opened again. Jon had slept for some time, but still felt cramped and physically exhausted.

Two leather-clad men armed with swords and knives stepped into the room. One threw down a leather harness which supported a sheath for sword and one for a knife; both were empty.

"Make yourself bare from the waist up," one of the men ordered gruffly. "Put on the harness. Fast. Lord Balt-Lot is not in the habit of being kept waiting for his entertainment."

"What about some food?" Jon asked, aware of the gnawing at the pit of his stomach.

"A dead man doesn't need food," the other warrior announced, grinning.

"If I had food, maybe I'd have a better chance of not being killed!" Jon started to remove the top of his now tattered silvery space uniform.

"You will be killed," the first man grunted. "Hurry. And shut up."

Jon took his time pulling off the top of his uniform. Then he slowly stood and picked up the harness. It was a belt supported by plain leather straps to fall over each shoulder, crisscrossing in front and back.

He strapped the harness over his own belt, which concealed the atomatic pellets. Jon considered using one of the explosives as a last resort, but immediately he realized this was impossible since there would not be time to nick the timer. No, they were only good for blowing his way through a wall, if it ever became necessary, or if he survived that long. There was, of course, always the chance that in the battle one of the pellets might be crushed or nicked even through the leather and thereby explode. But he had to take that chance.

The harness was in place.

"Come," the taller of the guards ordered. "We must hurry. Lord Balt-Lot is anxious to see a good fight."

As they started across the backyard toward the house, Jon thought about the other ships, and the people who might have survived the landing. What had been their fate? What would happen to Red and Mari? He could only find the answers to those questions by surviving long enough to search them out.

"You know," Jon said flippantly, "somehow I can't say I'm particularly anxious to get on with this show."

"What you think doesn't matter."

"To me it does."

The humorless guards retorted together. "Shut up."

Then the one on his left grunted. "It doesn't matter what you are anxious to do, or care about. You will die."

Next he was shoved into the house and to a large room in which some twenty people were all talking excitedly, obviously anxious to see the death-fight soon to follow.

Jon's first impression was that of entering a room in which a great classic play by some Federation Famous Author was about to start. The buzz and activity of people milling around the magnificently furnished room was almost exciting. Some of the guests clustered around the long wooden table laden with a feast of delicious looking food. The odor made Jon almost weak from hunger.

The room itself was some thirty feet wide and sixty feet long, with huge blue draperies hanging from floor to ceiling along all four walls. In the two far corners of the room were racks upon which hung an assortment of weapons, their purpose quite obvious.

Jon was ushered into the middle of the room. Lord Balt-Lot was perched behind the banquet table like some fat scavenger bird, a piece of meat clutched in his fist.

"Well, here's our star attraction!" he bellowed.

All eyes turned to Jon. There were snickers from the half dozen ladies in the group, dressed in long, flowing gowns which draped their figures in colorful folds.

"And where," shouted Lord Balt-Lot, "is my Champion?"

From the far end of the room, through another door, Londì appeared. He strode in quickly as if he had been awaiting the call from the Lord of the House of Balt-Lot.

"Well, we have our men. Let them begin." Lord Balt-Lot waved the chunk of greasy meat in the air in front of him. "And put on a good show. Londì, use the whip first. That's always good for a laugh or two. We could use a few laughs, couldn't we?" The last remark was aimed at his guests, who quickly murmured their approval, as if on cue.

Jon saw a face with a long scar running through right eye and cheek. Immediately he recognized Lorn-jan-dà, whose ugly features were contorted by a leering grin. The Raider had come to see him cut to death.

One of the men who had brought him to the room pushed Jon to the right wall. "Pick your weapon."

The sound of a whip snapping in the air some twenty feet alerted Jon to the fact that there would be no further ceremony. Already the guests had pressed themselves against the walls, making room for the combatants.

Jon studied the rack of weapons. There was a long black whip, neatly coiled. A knife, a long slender sword, a spiked mace on a chain, a long metal spear, and a huge wide-bladed axe.

He pulled the spear from the rack and leaned the weapon against the wall. He slipped the slender sword and knife into the sheaths at his waist.

Jon immediately realized that he had little chance with a whip; he knew nothing about handling one. The best bets would be the spear and knife. The spear could be used in the same manner as an atomatic rifle, using the weapon as a club or hand weapon. The knife was a simple matter, since he had fought with such a weapon many times.

Quickly Jon picked up the spear and examined it. It was one long piece of solid metal, quite light, and razor sharp at the point.

Turning, Jon gripped the spear with both hands, holding it at the middle and end. The blunt end of the weapon was set in position so that he could easily use it as a club or jabbing instrument. He knew it would be necessary to get in close and fast, so that the first blow could be struck against Londì.

The other man was already advancing.

The audience fell silent, afraid to miss one second of the drama. It seemed to Jon that his own breathing was the only sound in the room.

The whip moved like a long black snake behind Londì, alert, ready to strike, almost as if it contained some supernatural life of its own.

Jon took a deep breath, slowly shifting his weight. Then without warning he charged, zigzagging back and forth in an attempt to close the distance between himself and Londì before the whip could be put into effective use.

He was within five feet of Londì when the whip shot out, just missing his head as he moved to the right. The next moment Jon swung the butt of the spear toward the other's chin.

The solid impact would have broken a normal man's jaw, but Londì merely groaned as his head snapped back. His eyes registered surprise.

Jon slashed the point of the spear down and felt it cut across the other's chest.

The crowd roared its excitement at sight of the first blood to be drawn that evening.

Before Jon was able to jab the point of his spear into the gut of his opponent and put a quick end to the battle, Londì closed in fast. He grabbed Jon around the chest, knocking him off balance.

Jon felt himself falling backwards. His head hit the floor and for a dazed moment he didn't move. Then automatically his feet and arms gathered under him. Almost immediately he felt the impact of a foot in his face, downing him once more.

Jon lay there dazed, brain buzzing, vision blurred. For a moment he lost awareness of where he was. Then he felt the sting of the whip as it cut into the naked flesh of his back, and he remembered everything.

He had barely reacted to the pain, every muscle tensing, when another snapping sound brought a knife-like stab in his right arm. A third time the whip cracked, but not against his body, for Jon had already moved like some trapped cat, several feet away. He sprang to his feet, then felt pain wrap around his waist, pulling tight and biting deep.

Cursing, Jon tried to keep his balance, but the other man pulled, jerking him forward. Jon hit the floor. His nose felt as if it had been broken by the impact.

There was a roar of delight from the audience.

Jon heard footsteps moving away, then saw Londì pick up his fallen spear.

Still dazed, Jon managed to get to his feet as Londì started for him. The whip was still around his middle, but he ignored it. As he rushed forward, Jon slipped his sword out of its sheath and met Londì head on, swinging the light weapon in a downward arc. The blade met the spear shaft with a ringing sound.

Londì shot the butt of the spear toward Jon's head.

Jon ducked and came up under the other's arms, his left hand flattened and tensed to strike. The fingers jabbed toward Londì's exposed throat with all the strength of Jon's arm and the weight of his whole body behind it. But Londì's rushing bulk caught Jon unprepared. His hand missed the other's throat. A moment later he was falling backwards.

They tangled on the floor; for a moment it seemed Londì intended to kill with bare hands. Jon's guts exploded in pain as Londì's knee knocked the breath from him. Then he was alone with the pain, gasping for air.

Jon doubled up and writhed on the floor. His mind screamed that he must get up, arm himself before it was too late. Slowly, enveloped in pain, he managed to come to his feet. He watched through a red haze as Londì slid toward the wall rack and picked up the huge battle axe. It was at least two feet long, with a foot-wide blade.

Jon staggered to his own weapon rack, jerked his axe from its peg, and twisted around just in time to duck under a whistling slice from Londì's weapon. If it had connected, it would have cut him in two at the neck.

Coming up under the other's arms, Jon swung the handle of the axe into the steely muscles of Londì's stomach.

The man grunted and fell backward.

Jon's axe whipped through the air, just missing. Then Londì charged forward, axe swinging from left to right and aiming at Jon's middle.

Instead of ducking or sidestepping, Jon caught Londì's axe with his own. They stood panting, muscles straining, axes locked together.

The audience had been quite verbal in its excitement, but now fell silent. All eyes locked to the frozen struggle of the two men. It was a battle of nerve and muscle.

Jon watched Londì, saw the steely muscles knot. Beads of sweat formed on the other's forehead and ran down his cheeks.

The two men stared at one another for a long moment, then Jon saw something strange in Londì's expression. It was a mixture of fear and surprise and admiration. Londì seemed to be realizing that even the Champion of Lord Balt-Lot was not undefeatable.

Jon ducked, releasing the pressure on his axe.

Londì was thrown off balance by the sudden move. He fell forward, his axe slamming to the floor and biting deep. Jon kicked with his right foot, connecting with the side of Londì's head.

Londì rolled with the kick, twisted and sprang to his feet only a few inches from Jon's rack. Lightning fast, his right hand found the coiled whip, snaked it out and snapped it. The whip slapped around Jon's axe arm. His fingers went numb and the axe clattered loudly to the floor.

Londì pulled Jon's ball and chain quickly from the wall, swung it high over his head, and came charging forward, a low animal curse uttering from his lips. The wickedly spiked ball spun over his head.

Jon dove with outstretched arms and embraced Londì's legs, knocking him to the floor. A moment later both of them sprang to their feet, hands empty.

Londì backed away slightly, eyeing Jon's hands.

He had learned that afternoon that they could be deadly.

The men circled, then Londì whipped out his long knife and leaped forward. Ducking under the downward slash, Jon hit the other with a rabbit punch to the side of the neck and butted him in the chest with his head. Then Londì's knee smashed upward in a cruel blow to Jon's groin.

Red pain erupted through Jon's body. He felt something hammer at his jaw and then he was lying on the floor on his back, looking up at the business end of a descending axe.

Jon wasn't quite sure what had happened or how long he had been on his back. It couldn't have been more than a few seconds. But the battle was coming to a deadly end for him if he didn't move, and fast.

Jon rolled just as the axe blade sliced into the floor, so close that he felt the wind caress his right arm.

Jon kicked upward, both legs scissored in one quick motion, catching Londì at the knees and knocking the man face downward onto the floor. The sound of the huge body impacting resounded throughout the room.

The world spun, whirled and twisted around. Jon tried to get to his feet, fought to remain conscious, then suddenly black emptiness folded over him.

THE SLAVES OF LOMOORO, BY CHARLES NUETZEL

CHAPTER EIGHT

Training for the Arena

Jon was on his back in a darkened room. Hardly any sound came to his ears. For a long time he lay there, trying to figure out where he was. His body ached from the beating, but this he easily ignored. He was alive, and that was all that counted.

Jon sat up slowly and looked around in the semi-gloom. He began to make out shadows, and shortly after that he saw another bunk only a short distance away. A man was lying there, breathing heavily.

Jon stood on shaky feet and moved to the other bunk. Leaning over it, he examined the dim features of the large man lying there. It was Londì. He appeared to be unconscious.

Jon hesitated, then gently shook the other's shoulder. He wanted a lot of answers, and here was a man who might have them and be willing to talk.

Londì stirred and sat up. The man did not say anything for some time, but he was obviously trying to see who was standing over him. Then he grunted and threw his legs over the side of the bed.

"A good fight, friend," Londì offered gruffly. "We were both lucky. How do you feel?"

As the man spoke, his hands were fumbling with a small lamp on the floor. A few moments later, light flooded the room. Londì looked up at Jon and grinned. "You seem all right to me. I'm glad I did not kill you, for you are a great warrior."

The other's casual attitude surprised Jon. It was as if they had just finished a boxing match for the sport of some paying audience—but surely not a duel to the death. Half a dozen questions churned through his mind, but for some time he did not know where to start.

"Where are we?" Jon finally managed.

"In my quarters. No doubt you will now share them with me."

"What exactly happened—or do you know?" Jon decided not to wonder why he should be sharing Londì's room.

"Apparently you did not kill me." Londì grinned winningly. "For some reason Lord Balt-Lot decided that you might be more profitable to him alive than dead. From the fact that you are here in my room, I guess you will be trained to the Arena. There you will fight for the glory of the House of Balt-Lot and make Lord Balt-Lot much profit. If you survive long, you will someday be sold as some Lord's Champion—or replace me, if I should be killed." Londì was silent for a moment. "But I do not think you will be allowed to live for long. Lord Balt-Lot wants your woman, and he will do anything to get her!"

"Why doesn't he just kill me? Wouldn't that be much simpler?"

"It would also be against the law. If it ever got out that he killed the man of a female slave, he would be killed himself. You should know that. But I would nonetheless be watchful—a knife in the dark or an accident which would not be blamed upon Lord Balt-Lot could be arranged if he were willing to pay the price."

Jon immediately remembered Lorn-jan-dà. The man would be more than pleased to kill him.

"What makes you think I'll be trained to the Arena?" Jon asked.

"It will happen, for this is the way of Nal-Iò and Lord Balt-Lot. Once before a man survived death at one of the Master's parties—that man was myself. I did not kill the other, mainly because I was not able to. A lucky blow stopped him at the last moment. Then I lost consciousness from many bloody wounds. He had cut me to pieces. I still carry many scars. Later I awoke in the man's rooms, next to him. He taught me all that I know. Several years later he was killed and I replaced him as the Champion of the House of Balt-Lot. It is the way of Lord Balt-Lot!" Londi shrugged. "One cannot escape fate."

Jon shook his head. "One can change it."

"How? It is not the way of the gods. They point the finger at you and say it is your time. No matter what you do, there is no escaping."

"Then you believe there is no choice? You believe that whatever befalls you, the way is unchangeable?" Jon stared at the muscular giant.

"That is the way it is," Londi said.

"Well, for your information, I plan to live. And if it were possible, I would surely attempt to escape from this city." He said this last in such a way as not to bring too much suspicion on himself.

Londi laughed heartily. "It will not be possible to escape. Ever. If it were...Well, if I could have a different kind of life, if I were a Lord in my own city, maybe I would have gone a long time ago. You will learn and see how things really are. You will learn the truth!"

Jon shrugged and changed the subject. "If I wanted to discover the fate of some other people who had come in the same group of prisoners as myself, how would I go about it?"

"In time you will have free moments and then it is quite possible to go through the city as you wish, except for leaving the city walls or carrying weapons of any kind. But that might be ten days." Londi thought for a moment, then asked: "Whom do you wish to locate?"

"Two men who were brought here to Nal-Iò with me. Possibly they were sold to the Games. I don't know, because Balt-Lot bought us almost immediately."

"I will try to find them for you," Londi offered. "For we have fought together and lived. We are brothers in battle. You have my undying friendship. Whatever I can do, let me know." Londi reached out a large hand and placed it on Jon's shoulder. "I swear that if there is anything, I will willingly do it for you."

Jon immediately told Londì the names of his two friends. "I would like to see them, if it is possible. Could such a meeting be arranged?"

Londì nodded. "Perhaps, but I do not know when. Tomorrow I will ask about the slaves who were sold today. It shouldn't be hard to find out where they are and make arrangements to bring them to you, or you to them. We will see."

Jon thanked the other and without any further conversation Londì turned out the oil lamp and the two of them lay back on their bunks.

* * * * * * *

The next thing Jon knew, he was being roughly shaken by a leather-clad warrior.

"Food!" the man announced, still shaking Jon's arm. He put a bowl of warm, mushy substance on the floor. "Eat! Then change into these clothes."

The man placed a leather garment much like his own on the bed next to Jon. "There is not much time, for you are to begin training for the Games immediately after eating. Hurry!"

The man left and Jon reached for the bowl of strange food on the floor at his feet.

The mush tasted much like the meal which the Raiders had served before entering upon their last day's march to Nal-Iò. That was the last meal Jon had eaten. He realized now how hungry he'd been, and quickly finished off the food.

Afterward he felt better, and turned to the new clothing which had been brought for him. For a moment he hesitated, then slowly removed his gun belt and its precious atomatic pellets. There was a good chance that once he let the belt out of his possession, it would disappear for good. Hurriedly he removed the small wedge-shaped pellets and piled them on the bunk. He was nearly finished when footsteps sounded behind him. Jon palmed half a dozen pellets and turned to face one of his fellow slave-warriors—the man who had been there before.

"Are you not ready yet?" the man asked.

"Only a moment." Jon stood there waiting for the other to leave. When he did not do so, there was nothing to do but start undressing. As he threw his long pants onto the bed, Jon managed to slip the pellets from his hand under the thin mattress

"You had better hurry!" the man warned. "Geldo will be upset if we are late." His tone of voice was a little more friendly. "I hear you fought Londì and lived."

This last was stated with such admiration and disbelief that Jon turned and eyed the man more closely. He was not bad looking. Brown hair flowed over his shoulders in the fashion of the men of Nal-Iò.

Jon nodded. "I guess I was lucky."

"It had to be more than luck, for Londì is a great warrior. None have defeated him."

"What do I call you?" Jon asked, pulling on the g-string and harness which supported empty sheaths for sword and knife.

"Fal." The man reached out and touched Jon's right shoulder. "I hope you can be my friend."

It was now obvious to Jon that this action of touching another's shoulder was some formal gesture of friendship on Lomooro. He returned the same to Fal.

"I am Jon Handon."

"That is a strange name. Where do you come from?" Fal was now on a frankly companionable basis. It was as if the two of them had known each other for months.

"From...a long way off." Jon noticed that Fal was armed. He started to say more, then remembered the facts that Londì and Tanín had revealed to him about his origins; it was best to say nothing more. A few surprises might work to his advantage in the future.

Fal had taken Jon's explanation of his origin at face value. "Come," he said as Jon finished buckling his harness. "We must hurry."

Jon followed the other man down the corridor outside and into a huge room about twice the size of the one in which he and Londì had fought the night before. This room was some distance down the hall which seemed to be the pathway to all the slave-warrior quarters.

Half a dozen men were there before them. A man in a form-fitting blue robe which wrapped around his bulky body down to the knees, exposing heavy arms, was obviously in command. Jon guessed this would be Geldo.

Geldo jerked around and glared at Jon and Fal. "What kept you two?"

Fal said, "Jön-handön was sick."

"Jön-handön. What kind of name is that?" Geldo demanded. "No commoner has such a long name."

Jon shrugged. "Came to me at birth that way."

The other scowled, creasing his round fat face with deep lines. "Okay, Jön-handön. Join the group and do as instructed and we will get along fine. Get out of line and you will feel the sting of a whip across your back!"

In the next hours Geldo instructed the men in the arts of sword fighting. Most of those present already knew quite a bit. Jon began picking up the information quickly. The first lesson covered not only handling of the lightweight, extremely sharp sword which had been given to Jon, but the manner in which to defend oneself.

At first Geldo was miffed at Jon's ignorance, but by the end of the morning, Geldo was saying:

"You learn fast. In time you will be quite a swordsman." Not until later did Jon realize that this was a high compliment from the man. Geldo was not one to praise a student.

During the midday meal, Londì came into the room and stepped up to Jon. "I have found out what you wanted."

Jon wondered whether they should discuss the matter in front of Fal, who was eating next to him on one of the low benches lining the room.

"Where are they?" Jon asked.

"Both were bought by the Master of the Games. They are being trained into the Games Corps." Londì grinned like some little child who has discovered a delightful secret.

"Do you think I can see them someday?"

Fal laughed. Jon turned and looked at the young man questioningly.

"You know so little about the ways of this world, one would think you were new to it," Fal said. "Surely you come from some far place."

Londì nodded. "It would not be too hard to see them. After dinner some evening. I will talk to the Games Corps Master—maybe things can be arranged."

"Thanks."

"See you tonight." Londì turned and left the room.

The rest of the day they continued their swordsmanship lesson. Later Fal and Jon practiced together for some time. Fal was quite willing to help—teaching him how to handle a sword, answering all questions, no matter how simple. By the end of the day, though exhausted, Jon felt quite pleased with himself. Even Fal had openly exclaimed that he was doing well.

As they walked toward Jon's quarters, Fal said:

"It is truly hard to believe that you have never used a sword before. I know of no place—nor have I heard of such a place from another—where it is not necessary to know the art of the sword."

"We have other weapons in my land. But it would be impossible to explain to you." Jon stopped at the room he was sharing with Londì.

"You are truly a mighty warrior," Fal announced. "If you learn as fast every day as you did today, you will be a master. And you are truly lucky. I understand that, as custom orders, you will in time be trained by Londì."

"I have always been a soldier," Jon replied. "Maybe a man like myself has a natural skill in the art of fighting. I do not know. But I thank you for your help."

With that Jon stepped into the room and closed the door quickly behind him.

His first act was to see if his old clothing was still there. Surprisingly it lay on the bunk just as he had left it.

Hurriedly he began to empty the gun belt. He tore a strip of clothing from the pants, ripped the pockets out of them, and a few moments later he had strapped the pockets, with pellets tucked inside, into his Nal-Iò g-string, under the harness. Between them he was able to keep about twenty atomatic pellets. The others he hid under the mattress.

95

Jon sat on the edge of his bunk, trying to work out some plan for escape. But there were quite a few things to overcome before any kind of definite plan could be made. He would have to get Red, Mari and himself together, and then convince Tanín to come along. Otherwise there was little purpose in escaping, for one city on Lomooro would be much the same as another. Only Tanín could help.

Jon's thoughts were interrupted by the sound of heavy footsteps. Then the door opened and Londì entered the room.

The man approached Jon. "Day after tomorrow you will be able to meet with your friends," Londì said. "It has all been arranged."

* * * * * * *

How long Mari had been in the darkened room, she had no way of knowing. But apparently night had passed, and then morning, before the door opened. The woman called Penty stepped in and glared down at Mari with such evil hatred that a shiver shot through the prisoner.

"Well, little slave girl, have you learned your lesson?" The woman was armed with a small hand club which she looked quite able and willing to use. She wore a silken gown which was transparent, hiding only the more intimate portions of her body. The top strapped around her neck and dropped down over the back.

Mari did not need a second warning. Either she did what this woman ordered or it would go very hard upon her. She was half starved; her lips were cracked and dry. There was little doubt that another few days in this place would be too long.

Mari nodded and sat up on the small bunk.

"Okay, come. You will help with the washing, after you are given some decent clothing. And remember at all times that you are a maiden in the service of Lady Balt-Lot, and it is your duty to serve our mistress' every command. If you talk back to her, she will have you whipped—a pleasure I will gladly perform."

Mari quickly stood and followed Penty, who was obviously boss-girl of the chambermaids. Mari was given a piece of silken clothing which hardly covered her body.

"Change into this!" Penty ordered.

"What about something to eat?" Mari asked timidly.

Penty grinned. "At noon. You missed the early morning meal. That's what you get for sassing and attacking me. The next time you won't be so lucky."

As Mari reluctantly undressed, Penty glared at her. When she was completely naked, the woman made a face. "I don't know what the Master sees in you. But men will be... beasts. Women are their playthings."

Mari flushed. She quickly picked up the sheer white gown furnished by Penty and slipped into it. She felt almost as naked as before.

"Come!" Penty demanded, grabbing Mari by the arm and shoving her toward a door.

They went into another room, decorated much like the first. Here half a dozen girls dressed like herself were busy working. Some were cleaning clothes, and Penty ordered Mari to join them.

The next hours were taken up with washing the linens of the house of Balt-Lot. They were made of very fine material. Mari had seen nothing like them in the Federation Shopping Centers. The midday meal was Mari's first, and she was starved, weak almost to the point of fainting.

She overheard rumors about a fight which had taken place the night before and that Jön-handön, the new male slave, had survived against the Lord's Champion, Londì. Lord Balt-Lot had gone into a rage when the new slave was not killed. The girls giggled; they knew why his anger had been so great.

One of them looked at Mari. "He wanted to have you in his bed chambers last night. Your man is a mighty warrior to have survived a combat of death with Londì."

Because the guests had demanded it, Mari learned, Lord Balt-Lot had reluctantly and angrily instructed that Jön-handön be trained for the Arena. Mari could not quite understand why these people considered that an honor; from what she learned from the other girls, the Arena seemed a death trap.

The next day fell into a pattern which she was soon to

recognize as the daily routine of the chambermaids. Breakfast just before dawn, then housework around the large building in which Lord Balt-Lot lived. The house was U-shaped, with the living quarters at each end and the entertainment rooms in the middle. The men lived in the west wing and the female slaves in the east wing. Though she had hoped to see Jon Handon in the men's quarters, she was disappointed. She learned that the warrior-slaves were kept in a section which was off limits to the female slaves. She and her fellow slave girls would work all morning. After their noon meal, they would attend to the wishes of their Mistress, who was surprisingly attractive, though cruel and selfish.

Mari adjusted to the routine with little apparent difficulty.

* * * * * * *

Jon's next two days were repetitions of his first day in the House of Balt-Lot as a warrior-slave. He quickly learned that Geldo's routine was to use a different weapon each day. Through rotation, their instructor believed, one learned to be flexible in the use of all weapons. The battle axe, spear and sword all had a certain amount of common usage, and it was good to know how to defend oneself against each or any of them. One began to think in terms of how each weapon might best be used against the others. The whip, bow and arrow, and knife were different, and had little relation to the use of the other weapons. The apparent theory was to teach as much as possible, as fast as possible. The knowledge was urgently needed for, Jon learned, the Games came each ten-day.

The second day Jon trained with spears; the third with the battle axe. He was exhausted at the end of the lesson. As he went into the room he shared with Londì, he could think of nothing but rest. Not until he lay down on the bunk did he realize that this was the day he would meet with Red and Tanín.

Closing his eyes, Jon tried to ignore the aching of his muscles and get some rest before the evening meal and the reunion with his friends.

It seemed his eyes had hardly closed when a hand shook his shoulder.

"Jön-handön—wake up!" Londì's voice called through the darkness of sleep which had surrounded him so quickly.

Jon snapped upright, alert.

"We must hurry!" Londì urged.

"What's wrong?" Jon was completely awake now, standing.

"Nothing. But there is little time. You must move fast. You will have to meet the man you call Red during evening meal, since they are double training for the Games to take place within this ten-day!" Londì moved to the door. "Come."

Jon followed Londì; they made their way down the hall and out onto the darkened street. Jon felt a burst of exhilaration and a sense of freedom at breathing clear, clean air for the first time in days.

The sky was blood red on the eastern horizon; evening settled quickly upon the city of Nal-Iò. The streets were almost deserted.

Londì strode rapidly along the stone-paved streets toward the center of the city. The further they went, the shorter the blocks became. Finally Jon found himself standing in front of a magnificent circular building which was at least a thousand feet in diameter.

"This is the Arena," Londì explained. "This is where the Games are held. It is the exact center of the city."

Londì led the way across the wide road between the city buildings and the Arena. Jon now understood that the city of Nal-Iò was built like a huge pie. The streets cut toward the center, which was the Arena.

The Arena was fifty feet in height with large pillars upon which the figures of people were boldly sculptured in various positions—some endlessly looking out upon the street below, others holding weapons and bearing an expression of murderous hatred in their brooding eyes. These pillars were placed every twenty feet, each facing the entrance of a street. Between the pillars were arched doorways.

In the dim light Jon could make out more stone figures, armed, ready for battle, cut around these entrances. And as they came closer, he was amazed at the detailed workmanship of the sculptures.

Londì pushed open the huge wooden door and motioned for Jon to follow him. Once inside, the man closed the door behind them. They were in a passageway that led into an open Arena. Without invitation, Jon moved quickly to the other end of the corridor and found himself standing at the rim of a huge field surrounded by tiers upon tiers of benches. Jon imagined that the whole population of Nal-Iò could seat themselves at the Arena in one huge happy mass.

At each end of the field were large stone figures standing some twenty feet high, made of glittering silvery stone. They were the figures of two men, armed with swords, battle axes and shields, standing as if awaiting the command to begin a fight to the death.

Wind swept through the Arena, making a soft moaning sound as if the eerie voices of the thousands who had died here were crying out into the night. It was some time before Jon heard other sounds, far more alive, mingling with the night wind. They were soft, muffled, distant, but unmistakably those of some fearsome savage jungle beast. The moans seemed to come from the ground itself, under the Arena floor.

Looking up, Jon saw that the evening sky was sprinkled with multiple pinpoints of stars, splattered across the heavens from horizon to horizon like some whitish band which gathered almost into a solid mass of brightness toward zenith. It was alien and beautiful beyond words.

For some moments he stood there, looking up, listening to the moans of wild beasts and the wind that sounded like the cries of echoing voices from distant graves. Time seemed to freeze, and for those seconds of suspended time, Jon mentally bathed in a weird sensation that this savage, primitive Arena was the natural state of man, that this was the beginning and the end, from which it was impossible to escape. In that instant he could believe that the Galactic Empire did not exist, that he had been born on this world, that he was at home here among the Lomoorian savages.

Some seconds later Jon shook his head, looked down at the Arena floor again, and realized that this place, which might be the sports arena of some civilized city on one of the millions of worlds of the two Galactic Federations, in a way symbolized the whole human struggle since Adam and Eve. Man had come from the savage jungles of a planet called Earth and fought his way across the face of the world, into the skies and finally up across the reaches of space itself and into the infinities of the Galaxy and a million star systems. One solar system after another had been won by the blood of men's bodies. But Mankind continued onward, seeking new worlds to conquer, new horizons on which to spill blood.

His eyes swept the Arena. Here, he thought, the men of Lomooro fought a life and death struggle, as the two Federations were fighting a life and death struggle, with the citizens watching from the large video 3-D sets, enjoying conversations about it later with their friends at parties or work or play. There was little difference, and that was only in scope. Here a small Arena where people came and watched the actual blood being spilled, heard the actual screams of dying men. The murder was on a smaller scale, with only a few men dying. But on the Galactic scale it might be a city or a continent or a world or even a solar system that would suddenly stop existing at the press of a button. And, Jon realized, he had been one of the star actors in the drama of war and death and killing.

Then suddenly the moment shattered and was gone; with it had also gone Jon's own reaction of horror at the whole concept of the Games. Now he understood a little more about the people of Nal-Iò and the planet of Lomooro. He accepted things far more completely than before and could for the first time relate the society of Lomooro with that of his own. And he wondered if maybe these people were not just a little more honest in their approach to life.

"Come." Londì's voice broke softly into his thoughts. "Your friend Red will be waiting."

Jon turned, realizing that it had been but a few seconds since he had stepped to the edge of the Arena. It had seemed much longer.

He turned and followed the other man back along the

corridor to a small door which was hidden in the shadowy darkness surrounding them. Then they made their way down narrow stairs, lighted by the glow of gas lamps which hung every fifteen feet on the walls.

All Jon could think of was that they had to find some way to escape, some way to bring Red and Tanín out of this huge stone prison. Then, with Mari—and maybe Londì, too, if he wanted to go with them—escape the city of Nal-Iò forever. But first the meeting with Red. Then they would make their plans.

CHAPTER NINE

Sentenced to Death

Londì turned down a long corridor which was lighted in the same manner as the staircase above. Jon was able to hear the distant roar and cough of animals as he followed Londì under the Arena. Their footsteps echoed loudly against the stone floor; it seemed as if they were the only two people in the world. Suddenly they stopped in front of a stern looking, leather-clad guard.

The man stared grimly at Londì for a moment, then nodded. "They are in the cell. Down there—ten doors, on the left. Be quick about it."

Jon felt a cold chill rush over him as they moved around the guard. Finally they stopped in front of a small door. The loud sounds of men carrying on crude conversation came from within. Londì tapped and opened the door. He turned to look at Jon. "Wait there."

Without another word, Londì entered the room and closed the door behind him.

Jon waited in the corridor, aware that this obviously illegal meeting might be discovered. Then the door opened and Red Fendricks stepped out.

The two men gripped each other and grinned.

"Good seein' you!" Red exploded, pounding Jon on the back.

Jon nodded. "How are they treating you?"

"Can't complain, really, considerin' we're slaves and all that space rot." Red looked down at his huge hands. "Guess we're lucky to be alive. But I don't like the odds here. This Game thing. They're pretty rough."

"Still have the ammunition? The atomatic pellets?"

Red shook his head. "They took all our things the moment we were brought here."

Jon frowned. "Well, I managed to keep mine, at least. We have to find some way out of here."

Red shook his head again. "I've tried that. We're kept under guard all the time. Then after we have a workout, they put us down here. Once every ten-day they bring dancin' girls, wine and a feast – just before the Games. Guess they figure a guy should be goin' out happy."

"I thought you were supposed to win!" Jon countered, worried. "They say that anybody who goes up against the Games warriors is given little chance to live. If you win, you live."

"Until next time." Red made a wide gesture with beefy fists. "I don't like this setup in the least, even if it is rigged in our favor. If there was a way out, I'd jump at it. With the explosives we might blow our way out."

"Maybe something can be arranged so that all of us can escape," Jon said. "How's Tanín?"

"Fine. He's bein' trained somethin' special, so he's with another group right now. I don't know all that's goin' on. But we talked last night. When I explained that you have a means of gettin' us out of here, he said count him in, if possible. But it took some talkin'! These guys here just don't believe there's any chance to escape. Tanín half bought it when I explained how them explosives work. But he don't believe me, really. Sorta playin' along, I guess. Rockets, man, you'd think it was some sorta crime to want freedom!"

"Well, see how many of your fellow prisoners you can depend on going with us. See if there's any chance of taking a little army with us. Then we'd have a better chance of success," Jon suggested. "But don't let the others know that we are planning an escape. Just talk Tanín into advising you. Somehow, if I can get us all together, we might be able to give these people something to talk about for the rest of their lives. But it won't be easy."

Red had nodded silent agreement to everything Jon said.

Then he offered: "Well, I think there are a lot of guys willin' to spring the place, if they believed it was possible. But they have it in their brains that there's no way out. They accept this life with hardly a grumble!"

Red asked him how things had been going, and Jon told of the last few days. The other listened in silence. When Jon was finished, Red said: "You better watch out. I've heard some tales here. These rocket jammers think that life is nothin'. Killin' seems to be the trick for any problem."

"I know."

At that point Londì came from the cell. "We have to leave."

After a brief goodbye, Red disappeared into the cell.

Neither Jon nor Londì spoke until they were outside the Arena building and in the street. Then Jon asked: "How did you manage this for me?"

"A few favors," Londì admitted, grinning. "Normally it would be difficult. But I have a few friends here, from my days as an Arena warrior."

They made their way through the dark, silent streets and Jon found his mind forming hundreds of questions about the society in which he was now captive. Londì's friendship seemed impossible under the circumstances, yet there it was. Londì was a product of Lomoorian society, and his attitudes would surely be explained and understood once their society was understood.

Jon asked: "Do you really like your life here?"

"No, but what choice does a man have? He must accept things as they are."

"The choice of living for himself, being his own man, not owned and directed by others," Jon offered urgently.

"Is anybody ever his own man?" Londì asked.

"Okay. I'll admit nobody does exactly what he wants. But that's no reason to do what others tell you—even die— without even trying to change the situation. You would be better off fighting for some kind of existence out there in the jungle, all by yourself, than living as a slave for the rest of your life." Jon was already beginning to work out a plan to win Londì completely to his way of thinking. If that were possible, the man might prove to be the key to getting out of

Nal-Iò.

"You can't change Nature's way. The jungle is far more dangerous and deadly than the city," Londì explained. "And life is sweet—no matter what."

"That's not always true. Your life is not Nature's way. You were not meant to be a slave."

"There has been no other way on Lomooro," Londì stated matter-of-factly.

"In my land there is a different way. Every man may decide for himself what he wishes to be—and if he has any skill, any ability, he will get what he wants. At least he will be able to live with hope. A man without hope is hardly a man at all!" Jon saw that the other was seriously considering his words for the first time. "We do not have slaves. We do not have people dying at a man's command to provide entertainment for a party. We have our wars, but you do not have to be a soldier. And if you are, then that is something else—you picked it and so you have nothing to complain about."

"But such a world does not exist," Londì protested.

Jon considered for a moment. "Does it really matter? The important thing is that we make the most of our lives, and fight for what we believe in. And we must not sit back and let our freedom be taken from us by slave masters, simply because everybody says there is no way to change the system. I would rather die trying to obtain freedom than live under slavery."

Jon immediately regretted his last statement. In the heat of argument he had revealed all too clearly his true attitude, and now even Londì could guess what he might be planning.

But to Jon's amazement, Londì said: "I heard what you said to your friend. Is there really some way? Do you really have a magic that would make escape possible?"

The desperation in the man's voice was startling.

"I can escape if we have mounts, if I can get my friends all together. I promise you it is quite possible," Jon assured his friend.

"Then what? We leave Nal-Iò and death awaits us outside the city walls." But there was the sound of hope in Londì's voice. His large eyes were bright as he looked down into Jon's face.

"The Raiders survive, the Rals survive. And there is Tal-Jaÿ. One of my friends is very important in Tal-Jaÿ. If we returned him safely to his home, he would see to it that we received great honors and that we were accepted as friends. It is better than being a slave here, better than dying for nothing."

"What assurance would a man have that the people of Tal-Jaÿ would accept him as a friend?" Londì questioned as they turned down the side street that led to the House of Lord Balt-Lot. "Then I would be no better off than now. Possibly far worse."

"You might die in the next minute, Londì. We do not know if we will live to see the next day, do we? What assurance do you have that Balt-Lot won't order you killed or sent to the Arena to be killed someday? Or have one of the Raiders kill you? Or that the next man you are asked to fight might not be more skilled—or have unexpected luck—and kill you. It almost happened with the two of us. A thin edge between life and death. It is too precious to play games with, and you know it. Someday you will be killed. You will slip. One mistake, and that will be the end of you."

They had stopped outside the House of Balt-Lot. Facing each other in the darkness, Jon was able to make out Londì's expression of puzzlement. "As things now stand, you have no hope," Jon persisted. "If you were to escape, at least there would be some hope. There would be a chance for a better way of life."

The ideas were apparently new to Londì and he seemed to be struggling to accept them. After some moments, Londì shrugged. "But it is all merely talk, since it is impossible. However, I will not say anything about your plans, since they will not be put into action anyway. You will learn. I truly wish it were possible. I wish that you were not a little mad."

Jon sighed. "What if I could prove that I had great magic?"

"Ah, that would be different. But of course," Londì grinned, pleased with himself, "there is no such thing as magic, is there?"

Jon found it hard to keep from agreeing with the man, since he truly knew there was no such thing. But in the eyes of Londì and the others from Lomooro, almost any modern invention would seem magical.

"Yet," Jon offered, "if there were, if I could prove it to you, then everything would be different?"

"I only wish it were so!" Londì opened the side door which led to the slaves' quarters. "Many would follow such a man who could do magic."

As the two men moved into the house, Jon asked, "Have you heard anything about the woman brought here with me?"

"Your woman?" Londì closed the door behind them.

"Yes."

"She is well. She is a servant girl for the Mistress Balt-Lot, as you know. If you wish, I could arrange a meeting with her for you." Londì said this as they stepped into their small room. "It could be dangerous, but I know Penty. She would do anything for me."

"Is she being well treated?" Jon sat on his bunk.

"If you mean will Lord Balt-Lot touch her—not as long as you live."

Jon sighed and leaned back on the bunk. He half closed his eyes and considered half a dozen possible plans of escape. If Londì would only become convinced that escape was possible and that freedom would be far more rewarding than the life he now led, things might be much easier.

The next day Londì told Jon that it would not be long before he would be instructing Jon in the Art of Combat. "I understand that you are doing wonderfully."

Jon had spent a hard afternoon learning how to handle a whip—an art which turned out to be quite demanding and difficult to learn. The whole idea of learning how to fight in some primitive life-and-death games for the pleasure of the populace held little fascination.

Jon asked the man about arranging a meeting with Mari, and was told it might be done the next night.

In the conversation which followed, Jon asked Londì about the difference between being sent to the Arena as a warrior, and being sentenced to the Arena for some crime against the city of Nal-Iò.

"When you are sent as a warrior," Londì explained, "you might fight with another man, as you did that first evening with me. But if you are sentenced, it will be sure death because you will be pitted against a Lombor, Lients or Palt— one, or two together, or three all at once. You would be totally unarmed. It might be a single animal or it might be a dozen. It depends on the crime. If they want it to be a slow death, they have devised some nice ways of killing a man or woman so that it will be quite entertaining for the audience. But that is another matter." Londì spread his hands wide. "As a warrior, I think you will survive many combats. You will become a hero and bring a lot of Tals to Lord Balt-Lot's home."

Londì stood. "I have drawn extra duty tonight, my friend. Our Master is a guest at the home of Lord Yaat for dinner, and wants me to put on a show for them. I will probably be late."

After Londì had left their sleeping quarters, Jon found himself musing over the fact that in the beginning his only real thought had been to locate another of the scout-boats and find a way off the Planet of Lomooro. Now it had become simple escape from unfriendly captors in the hopes that they would find friends on this world in the city of Tal-Jaÿ. The idea of escaping from the planet itself seemed quite distant and unreal. If anyone had landed in the scout-boats and survived, it seemed unlikely they would remain free very long. Yet his own companions were still alive, so far at least. This was really all that mattered. In time, if life held out, escape might be possible.

Jon turned off the oil lamp and settled back in the bunk. For a long time he lay there in the solitary darkness, working out details of possible escape plans. All of them seemed unworkable after short examination, for they all relied upon escaping by their own efforts. They needed help. If he had help, it might be possible to free Tanín and Red from the Arena Master, get Mari, and blast their way out of the city with the explosive pellets. With mounts it might be possible to make it down the cliff ledge and into the jungle below before any real organized pursuit could be started. If they were not killed by some arrow or spear. But they needed help.

Jon fell into a troubled sleep. Then his mind suddenly snapped awake, aware of danger looming nearby.

He froze.

Somebody was in the room. He felt the presence like some evil force reaching out to attack, to kill, to strike without warning.

For some time he lay there in the darkness, unmoving, feigning sleep while his mind conjured up more horrible dangers than could have existed in the normal universe. Blackness ebbed around him, pressing inward with invisible hands choking at his senses until every nerve was alert, waiting for swift and terrible death.

Padded feet slipped across the floor. Another person was in the room besides himself—someone determined to kill. Jon opened his eyes carefully and peered into the gloomy darkness.

A huge shadowy form was looming over the bed, not a yard away. Jon's muscles tightened, ready to fend off any attack. The mysterious visitor seemed to sense that Jon was awake. For a moment it hung there, then with a bestial curse the shadow leaped forward. Something flashed down toward Jon's chest in a gleaming arc designed to cut into his flesh, to cut away life.

Jon's body reacted like a well-programmed machine. Right hand reached up and found the other's wrist as it plunged downward; left fist slammed out, smashing into hard stomach muscles.

A yell of pain pierced the room like an exploding rocket tube screaming against the agony of takeoff.

As his knee jerked up, Jon struck down with his right hand against the back of the man's neck. Between the force of hand and knee, both making contact from opposite directions, the other's neck broke like the snapping of a rocket hull under fire of an atomatic cannon. Without another sound, Jon's would-be killer slumped to the floor, dead.

A second later Jon turned on the lamp and looked at the body lying on the stone floor.

The man was on his stomach and had to be turned before

Jon could see the scarred face. But even as he pushed the body with the point of his foot, Jon knew who it was. Lorn-jan-dà.

Jon sighed and wondered what he would do with the body. Then suddenly the door of the room burst open. Fal rushed in, followed by half a dozen other warriors.

"What happened?" Fal asked, eyes wide at sight of the dead Raider.

"He tried to kill me."

One of the other men grunted. "Well, that's the end of you."

"What does he mean?" Jon demanded of Fal, who had been friendly since their first meeting.

The Lomoorian looked unhappy. "No slave may kill another man, unless that man also be a slave."

Jon exploded in horror. "But the man tried to kill me!"

"That does not matter."

"What should I have done—let him kill me?"

"It might have been a quicker death!" Fal admitted. "You may wish it had been that, once you face the Lients in the Arena."

One of the other men took charge at this point. "Take the body out! Put this man under guard. Bolt the door! We will await the arrival of Lord Balt-Lot!"

As the others removed the body of Lorn-jan-dà from the room, Fal told him, "Lord Balt-Lot might not report this. It is his choice to make. He will probably see that it is foolish to train such a grand warrior only to let him become meat for the Lients. It is completely up to the Master."

Jon realized that the words were meant to be encouraging, but their effect was quite the opposite.

The door finally closed and he heard the bolt shot into place.

Jon paced the floor, thinking about the possibility of blowing his way out of the room with one of the atomatic pellets. Then he realized this was impossible; the charge going off in such cramped quarters would probably also kill him. If he had an atomatic blaster, it would have been different. Going into the body of a man, as it would when shot from a gun, the explosion would be absorbed by flesh and bone. Going into a wooden panel, it would get the same result, with the blast going outward. But when thrown, the pellet spent its force in all directions at once, limiting its use.

Jon believed that the death sentence would be automatic under the circumstances. Some time later he proved to be correct. Lord Balt-Lot had not overlooked his golden chance to rid himself of the one man who stood between him and the new female slave. The door was unbolted; four guards with drawn swords stepped into the small room.

"Come! To the dungeons with you!" said the man in charge, a huge brute of a fellow with thick muscular arms and a bull neck.

"I take it I won't be having a trial?" Jon inquired, not moving from the bunk.

"You had your trial. You're sentenced to the next Games." The man laughed coarsely, followed immediately by his fellows.

"Come on, don't cause any trouble and you'll have a few more days of life."

With that the man pressed his sword into the small of Jon's back. In moments he was being ushered down a long gloomy staircase which went some distance below ground before ending in front of a large metal door. The man in charge unlocked the door, opened it and ordered his prisoner inside. A moment later Jon was in total darkness.

A quick exploration revealed that he was in a small, damp cell

There was nothing left to do but lie down on the cold, hard, stone floor and await coming events. What little chance there had been to escape had now totally disappeared. They were all doomed. If he had given Red the atomatic pellets— at least a few—then there might have been some chance for Mari. Now it seemed certain that death awaited all three of them.

* * * * * * *

It might have been an hour, a day, two days, Jon had no way of knowing, for in this black pit no light of any kind filtered through. He slept and awoke later, but with no sense of reality. When he opened his eyes, it seemed as if he were buried. An oppressive fear ate at him until the immediate cloud of sleep passed, and awareness returned.

Dryness seared his throat and his stomach churned with hunger. These pangs suggested that he had been sleeping for a long time.

Jon slowly stood. He paced off the width and breadth of the cell—three and a half large steps. He continued moving back and forth in order to keep his muscles in top condition. In the beginning he counted the turns, then lost track. Some time later footsteps sounded outside and a small panel opened near the bottom of the door.

Jon squinted against the brightness which flooded into the cell as a little tray was slipped through the panel. When darkness had again folded around him, Jon reached greedily for the bowl which he had seen on the tray. He reached toward where the tray had been just before light had disappeared. He found the earthenware; as he raised it to his mouth, some of the soupy contents spilled onto the floor. Like a starved animal, he started to gulp.

After the first couple of swallows, Jon hesitated, then ate more slowly, controlling the anxious grind at the pit of his stomach. Some time later he put the empty bowl on the tray.

He slept, paced the cell, and slept again before food was brought once more. His empty bowl and tray were not removed until the guard brought new food.

The only indication of passing time was the fact that his stomach was sick from hunger, his mouth like a burning desert. This time Jon drank only half the soupy food, keeping the rest for later. Then he once more began pacing around the small cell.

Another man in his situation might have quickly broken under the pressure of total darkness, no real awareness of time's passage, and knowledge that in only a matter of days he would face death in some primitive Arena for the thrill and pleasure of a city of near-savages. As far as Jon knew, it might only be moments before they would come and take him to the Arena. Time had no actual meaning other than the pacing, the count, the cadence of his feet stepping, turning, stepping, turning, around and around until his brain reeled.

113

Then Jon sat down on the hard floor. Only the years of training in the Space Service kept Jon's mind and spirit and hope from shriveling and dying inside him.

His thoughts turned to Mari and Red and Tanín, wondering if there was any hope for them. Probably more hope than for himself.

Food was brought once more. Jon was pacing back and forth in his cell when the door suddenly burst open. For a moment he continued pacing like some dumb animal gone insane, treading around and around, unable to stop, unaware of his surroundings.

A voice ordered him out of the cell. For some moments he stood there, blinded by the glaring light.

"Come on! Hurry, man!" another voice ordered nastily, as the guard pricked Jon's back with the point of his sword. "We can't keep the Games Master waiting!"

* * * * * * *

When Mari was awakened in the women's slave quarters just off Mistress Balt-Lot's room, she felt a sense of doom cut through her like a knife. The night before, word had come that the new male slave was to be killed in the Arena the next day for having murdered the Raider Lorn-jan-dà of the Jan-dà tribe.

Her eyes opened, then she heard the sound of morning conversation. But all this blended into the background, for in the shadowy darkness of the pre-dawn she felt the presence of Penty like some evil spirit above her.

"Tonight, girl! You will know what it is to be a woman of Lord Balt-Lot!" Rough hands grabbed Mari from both sides. "We must get you prepared!" Then she was lifted from the small bunk.

In the hours that followed, Mari was bathed in perfumed waters in the Mistress' large bath. Beautiful silken gowns of yellow, red and orange were brought, and she was dressed in the soft transparent material which fell around her body in misty waves.

Penty, who was in charge of the female slaves attending to Mari, leered at her. "You will do!"

Penty pushed Mari toward the only exit from the room. "Come, woman! You must be ready for the Master."

In silence Mari was escorted by half a dozen girls down a hallway and to a door which was opened for her.

Penty shoved Mari inside. "You will wait here for the Master's pleasure. After your man has been fed to the Lients, you will become Lord Balt-Lot's!"

The door slammed shut and was bolted.

Mari looked around and found herself in a large bed chamber. The bed was huge—big enough for several couples to lie upon. On each side was a stand with a huge, beautifully painted vase. But Mari could not appreciate the elegance.

She crumpled to the floor beside the bed, sobbing, every nerve raw with defeat and terror.

Several days ago she had heard the rumor about Lorn-jan-dà visiting Lord Balt-Lot. That same day, the man was killed by Jon. But even with the death sentence hanging over him, it had all seemed unreal to Mari. Somehow Jon Handon would find a means of escaping.

But now, in the room in which Lord Balt-Lot expected to take her to bed, Mari felt the total defeat press upon her with an overwhelming force which she was unable to bear.

Jon Handon was to be killed, and Lord Balt-Lot was to have his female slave to do his bidding. And there was nothing anybody could do to stop it.

THE SLAVES OF LOMOORO, BY CHARLES NUETZEL

CHAPTER TEN

The Games

Slowly Jon's eyes became accustomed to the brightness which flooded through the open door of his cell. He made out the figures of two warriors, dressed in black leather uniforms much like those of the House of Balt-Lot, though more detailed in the designs tooled into the darkened leather. These men were total strangers.

"Where now?" Jon stepped from the cell, his eyes still hurting from the light.

One of the men pushed him toward the staircase. "Quiet!" Jon felt the sharp prick of a sword touch the middle of his back.

Jon finally was shoved outside the House of Balt-Lot and into the streets of Nal-Iò, where two other guards awaited their arrival. They flanked Jon on both sides and the group slowly made its way through the totally deserted city streets. The only sound was the soft moaning of one of the many house pets, a *topì,* which reminded Jon of the earth dogs which were popular house pets in the Sol sector of the Galactic Federation. These Lomoorian house pets were earless and far more deadly looking, with large fangs and upturned tusks which stood out about three inches from their lower lips and jaw. Yet he understood that they were quite friendly, and seldom would hurt humans, even when attacked.

"Where is everybody?" Jon asked as they made their way along the silent streets toward the center of town and the

Games Arena.

"The Games, fool!" a guard snapped. "Now, quiet!"

Jon felt nausea squeeze the pit of his stomach into a tight lump of pain. It was not so much the idea of facing death, but that it must be done in front of thousands of people. Death was so personal a thing. Even in the midst of war it became personal—and one did not want it intruded upon by any more people than necessary.

He thought about the Long Wars between the Galactic Federations, and now found it difficult to believe in their importance. What had seemed so vital before coming to Lomooro now seemed distantly childish. The only really important thing was personal survival. The idea of life after death was something Jon had never really considered seriously The business of war had been far more important in the Handon household. Death was the end product of not being the winner in mortal combat. Death was for losers. What took place after death was a mystery which neither his father nor his mother had attempted to explain in any detail. Jon had never given much thought to it, but now, walking through the streets of Nal-Iò, he considered death and rejected it. He would face it later, some other time—in the distant future. Yet he was not afraid of it. Every thought, every moment of living had been centered on the art of combat, of killing, of war, for there always had to be those in the universe who would fight for freedom and peace.

After some ten minutes the group came to the large circular Arena, from which Jon could hear throaty shouts of excitement.

A shudder rushed through him as he followed the escort into the Games building and down a dimly lit corridor. He was led below the Arena floor, not far from where Londi had taken him some days before. From here Jon could hear the screams of animals gone wild with rage and killing, the yells of terror of dying people.

His four guards took him along the corridor for some hundred feet and then made a left turn down another stone hallway. In moments they came to a barred metal door, before which two warriors stood guard over some twenty men and women.

"Another for your pen!" one of Jon's guards announced. "The prisoner-slave from Lord Balt-Lot. He is to face the Lients."

As he was pushed into the cell with the other prisoners, Jon heard one of the men say: "He's a mad one for sure. Days in darkness, walking back and forth in his cell. A mad one who will not even know he is dying."

"Well, the Lients will make quick work of him!" a guard grunted as the escort turned and went back down the hall.

Jon looked at the other prisoners, wondering what their crimes had been.

They all had the same distant, haunted look; for some time Jon could not quite understand it. Then slowly he realized that the expression was one of disbelief—they could not quite understand how and why they were here or that they were about to die. Nobody could really imagine their own end, their own death.

Jon turned to a man standing nearby against a stone wall. "What happens next?"

The fellow gazed at Jon as if he were seeing some kind of freak. "You should know as well as the rest of us."

"I am new to Nal-Iò."

"Is it not the same all over Lomooro?" the man asked. "You do something different—something which is against the Law—and you end up here in this room, spending the last moments of your life in holy terror. We will all be dead. It is merely a matter of a short while. They will take us from here to our death. You wait. You watch. You will see."

The man's face was lined, his hair gray, his lips thin. Age and hopelessness etched his features.

"Maybe we will live," Jon suggested, trying to offer the other some kind of hope, no matter how remote.

"We will die!" the man screamed. "And Hell itself will burn fires of agony through the bones of our souls! We will not be saved! So why hope? Why believe in anything other than the fact that death is here—as it has been for hundreds of others in the past. We will all die, and the meat of our bodies will feed the Arena beasts. The ground will be wet with our blood long after the last screams of dying agony have left tortured lips."

The man's eyes grew large and glassy as he spoke; his mouth quivered with each word. "We will all be blood on the ground! Death like a rot smelling the air—and it will be our lives, our moments of joy and hate, happiness and fear, thoughts, love—all torn in one instant from our bodies. Years of living, years of struggling from one moment to the next—all ended in the violence of an unnatural death. A bloody, unnatural death."

Gradually the man's tense body relaxed and a twisted smile formed on his thin lips. "I am sorry." His voice was small and tired.

The others in the cell had moved close to see the raving man. They murmured in understanding and agreement.

Jon turned, studying his fellow prisoners now that their attention was centered on the old man. Most of them looked too weak to put up a good fight in the Arena. They were weakened by lives fed with fat, with ease, supported by the labors of a slave society. Yet in their haunted eyes there was the look of men who did not like the life they had led, had not enjoyed the trap into which their society had pushed them. Still, they did not want to die. The fear dug deep into their features, twisting in haggard lines.

Jon became aware that fear, more than anything else, made the people of Lomooro willing to keep things as they were. To attempt change would surely mean death. Death faced them all in the Arena for whatever crimes they had been a party to, and probably even if they only spoke against the system.

"There is nothing we can do," the man mumbled. "We have all stood for equality—for the right to speak our minds. We do not want to die. Yet in our dying maybe there will be hope."

The man stood straight again and looked at the others in the cell with him. Jon realized that these people probably belonged to a special group who had been placed here together for a mutual crime.

The man continued. "Hope of a better life, a better world! Maybe somebody will remember what we have tried to do. Remember why we die here."

One of the guards pounded the cell bars with his spear.

"Shut up, old man! Nobody will remember you—none will remember any of you. You are all crazy! Even crazier than the slave from Lord Balt-Lot! Shut up!"

The old man glared at the guard, but he lapsed into silence. The others around them just stood, looking at the ground at their feet, defeated.

Jon asked all of them, but particularly the old man, "What have you been sentenced here for?"

The man looked at Jon and seemed to see him for the first time. "Why? Because we wanted to bring an end to this very thing: the Games. We believe life is something special—that the Old God, the One God, created life and that it is not for us to kill that which God created. We are not believers in murder and killing."

"It is man's way to kill," Jon pointed out gently. "I have studied Mankind. As he traveled throughout the universe, he found conflict and found it necessary to fight for survival – others and his own." Jon stated this matter-of-factly. "Surely you will not die without fighting?"

The old man stared at Jon, eyes unwavering. "We will die unnatural deaths. As you say, it is the way of man to kill, but it is not right. Man can change—if he wants to. It says in the Old Book that there are Gods in Heaven and that they will come some day to our world and take us to a new place where there are many, many worlds like this one. I do not understand all that is written in the Old Book, but I do believe it, for so it was written by the First Captain. We must believe, without really knowing."

Jon felt as if an electric shock had shot through him. "The Old Book you speak of—what is it?"

"It tells of a strange trip across the darkness. It tells of coming out of the darkness to Lomooro and living. It tells of how we were saved by the goodness of Lomooro where there was light and darkness, where there was water and food. One does not question the Gods. One does not try to understand that which is not understandable to the mind of man. But we believe! And it says in the Old Book that man should not kill! Yet we have forgotten the wise words of the Old Book for all too long and..."

One of the guards opened the barred door, bringing the

121

old man's words to a halt.

Jon silently cursed the guard. He wanted to hear more, wanted to question the man further. It was obvious to him that the Old Book was some kind of ship's log or record of legend, and would tell much about the original inhabitants of Lomooro, reveal from whence they had come and how long ago. He was convinced now that he was in with a group of Lomoorian fanatics, but the old man's belief was certainly an indication that there were people on Lomooro who would like to have things changed, who did not like the status quo.

For the first time, Jon Handon gave thought to what he might want to do if he were trapped on this planet for the rest of his life—assuming he survived the next hour.

"Come!" the guard ordered, indicating all of them. "You will be taken to the Arena now."

The old man nodded, as if to himself. "So let it be."

Jon wanted to continue talking with the man, but it was quite impossible. The guards shoved and prodded anybody within reach of arm or spear, forcing them down the stone corridor.

They continued for some twenty yards and then made a turn. Facing them was a large arched opening, barred at the end, beyond which could be seen the Arena itself. They were herded into the end of this corridor; a gate lowered between them and the guards.

"Have fun!" one of the guards taunted.

Suddenly the bars which stood between them and the Arena creaked upward. A guard yelled:

"Go on out or we will send arrows into your cowardly backs!"

As the prisoners hesitated, one of the guards sank an arrow into the back of a man only a couple of feet from Jon.

It was all that was necessary. The others started to move out into the Arena. Jon caught the dead form of his fellow prisoner and dragged the man into the Arena. He moved to one side, away from the entrance, so there would be no chance of being shot by one of the Nal-Iò guards. Then he lay the body on the ground and jerked the arrow from the poor fellow's back. He snapped the arrow two inches from its metal tip and dropped the feathered end. He palmed the arrow, then turned his attention to his surroundings as the gate under which the prisoners had passed slowly slid back into place.

His immediate reaction upon seeing the Arena was one of shock. The place exuded a sense of almost pagan excitement. He had seen the place once before, during the night, and the shadows of night had coupled with the nakedness of the bleachers to create an illusion of loneliness, of being lost in the middle of Space or in some timeless dimension where history looked back and mocked itself.

What surrounded him now was completely different— alive and crowded to the brim with laughing, shouting people of all ages.

Pennants waved gaily in the sunlight. Their designs were varies—needles, spears, crosses checks and circles— and were set every ten feet around the top of the Arena wall. Excited voice merged thunderously, the sound itself radiating all awareness of moment, a feeling that what was happening was important and had meaning – a moment of destiny.

At one end of the Arena was a large sector somewhat different from the rest of the bleachers. Here was glory carved in golden colors, splattered in vivid reds and yellows, crowned by a covering of silvery plating. Here would be the High Captain of Nal-Iò and his Royal Court. The splendor of the High Captain's immediate surroundings reached out to Jon and touched him with excitement, as it was meant to do to the warriors of Nal-Iò in the service of their City. It was savage, but sparkling with radiant power which cries for others to follow, no matter what the command.

Jon made a quick sweep of the area with his eyes. He turned slowly, taking in the huge statue-warriors sparkling in the bright sunlight; they almost seemed alive, so great was the detail, so fine the artistry which had created them.

Jon's companions had moved like sheep to the center of the huge Arena. They gathered together. The white-haired man fell to his knees, raising his hands to the sky, to the sun itself. His lips moved, but even from the distance of a mere twenty feet, Jon could not hear the man's voice.

A roar of contempt shuddered through the audience,

rippling around and around like a living thing.

Jon quickly reached under his loin cloth and pulled out one of the pocket-bags he had made some time before. Opening it, he extracted five atomatic pellets, one of which he held between thumb and forefinger of his right hand. Then Jon moved toward the other prisoners, coming to a stop before the group just as its members fell to their knees, following the example of their leader.

Jon decided to ignore them completely. He stood ready, the metal tip of the arrow poised close to the soft portion of the wedge-shaped explosive pellet in his right hand.

Suddenly a spear rose from the High Captain's section, held aloft by an ornately dressed officer. Trumpets sounded from four corners of the Arena.

Jon's body tensed, ready for whatever death might be offered.

As the sound of trumpets faded, silence fell over the audience. The quiet was far more terrible than the excitement which had drummed the air around them before. Everybody in the Arena seemed to have stopped breathing in anticipation of the bloody orgy of death about to take place before their eyes.

During these moments Jon felt alone. There were people behind him, silently waiting for death to choke their lives away; others watched for the show of blood to begin. Yet he felt as if he stood alone in the world, in the whole universe, ready to face his Maker—or win the day. His muscles, his training, his mind, might save life. Nobody would help him. The others would die without a fight. He held in his hands the possible means of survival. Five tiny pellets

There was a timeless moment, then metal grated on metal and the low coughing from the throats of jungle beasts came to him, bringing an end to the waiting.

From a dozen dark openings in the Arena wall, huge horrible looking beasts came slinking into the sunlight. Jon stared. They were like hairless cats, at least twice the size of a man. Eight legs supported each huge body, ending in long clawed feet. Their heads were large, containing saber-like fangs six inches long. Their bodies were covered with hairless tan hide which wrinkled as they moved.

Jon heard a low rumble which sent a shiver from the base of his neck to the lowest point of his spine. He turned. One of the beasts—which he had recognized from descriptions given him by Tanín as Lients—came charging at a fantastic speed into the middle of the group of defenseless men. They screamed in terror, scattering in all directions. Jon could now understand why they had given up even before entering the Arena. What chance did an unarmed man have against such savage creatures?

Jaws crunched together over the head and shoulders of one man, cutting the poor fellow's neck in two. Blood splattered in every direction, covering the Lient's soft hide. Then beasts and humans were darting madly all around the Arena like characters in some grotesque comedy.

Jon saw one of the beasts start in his direction. Ice settled at the pit of his stomach. His fingers moved, pressing the point of the arrow into the atomatic pellet, cutting the timer which opened the explosive to its catalyst—oxygen. Then he drew back his right arm and threw the explosive at the oncoming beast.

For what could not have been more than a split second but seemed far longer, Jon waited, breathless, aware of everything around him. Sight, sound, smell attacked his senses. The hot breath of the beasts filled the air like some choking sick poison. The sound from the bloodthirsty audience was now a roar that continued up and down the scale as if attempting to drown out the growls of beasts and the dying screams of men and women being torn or crushed under the giant jaws and claws of the Lients.

Jon had never before tried throwing the explosives. The savage Lomoorians must be expert in driving a spear point into the heart of a man at twenty paces, but the necessity of hitting his target was less crucial. The explosive charge would be almost as effective in frightening the beasts as in killing them. But, to save his life, he would have to kill.

Then suddenly an explosive brightness blasted between him and the leaping Lients not ten feet away. One beast screamed in agony. Jon needed no further evidence that his aim had been perfect. The creature fell to the Arena floor, convulsing wildly in pain, though far from death.

Jon didn't watch the Lients, but immediately took in the scene surrounding him. His fellow prisoners were at the far corners of the Arena. There was now a heavy silence. Many spectators were standing. All eyes had turned to the center of the Arena, where Jon now stood a short distance from the convulsing Lient. He could well imagine the shocked surprise of the spectators. They had not expected death to reach out and touch their Arena beasts.

Jon surveyed the mass slaughter in the Arena, his mind groping for some means of escape. There were far too many Lients surrounding him—it would be impossible to kill all of them. Retreat was the only alternative.

Jon searched for some way out of the death trap in which he now found himself. The walls were far too high to climb, but there were several barred exits much like the one through which he had been forced to enter the Arena.

Jon made his decision and started toward the nearest gate, some twenty yards away. A roar came from the audience as they guessed his plan. A Lient stood from his kill and saw Jon running. The beast came to its feet so quickly that Jon could hardly believe his eyes. He immediately stopped, nicked another explosive pellet, held his breath and threw it toward the charging animal.

Jon raced toward the gate, reaching it just as the sound of the explosive roared through the Arena, followed by a frenzied yell from the spectators.

Jon pressed the slim point of the arrow into another pellet, placed the tiny explosive in the center of the barred gate, then stepped to one side and flattened against the wall.

His eyes scanned the Arena. All his fellow captives had already been killed. The Lients were feasting upon the bloody brushed bodies of their kills. He felt a shudder rush through him, then an explosion shook the wall. Metal blasted from the doorway and out onto the Arena floor.

Jon rushed through the twisted remains of the metal gate. In his right fist he still carried the two remaining explosives, in his left was the small arrow. He half expected to run into armed warriors, but as he moved into the gloomy darkness of the corridor, he found it was totally empty except for himself, and silent but for his footsteps.

Jon stopped long enough to put the two explosive pellets into the pocket-pouch under his loin cloth. Then, holding the arrow in his right hand much like a small knife, he continued along the dim corridor, every moment expecting sounds of pursuit.

Jon realized that the moment he ran into armed guards there would be little chance of keeping his life for very long. Unarmed as he was, and for the most part unskilled in use of the primitive weapons of the people of Lomooro, he could hardly hope to survive. But such death, fighting men, would be far better than dying under the fangs of the Lients.

The corridor abruptly turned left. As Jon started to move in this new direction, the sound of pounding feet came from behind. A shiver sickened him. He hesitated for only a moment, then rushed blindly along the corridor. One thought motivated him: to put as much distance as possible between himself and the Lient which was now following him.

It was some moments before he heard the clanking of metal against stone, up ahead. When he realized the significance of the sound, Jon felt a sudden sense of hopelessness. There might have been some slight chance of escaping the fangs of the Lients, but now there was no hope at all.

What little moments might have been won were now narrowed down to mere seconds. Trapped between savage beast and savage armed warriors, there was no hope at all. His mad flight for freedom had been useless. How could he hope to outfight beast and man coming from different ends of the corridor? How could he hope to escape? His mind spun in total defeat. It was going to end for him here—in the corridors under the Arena in the city of Nal-Iò on a lost planet called Lomooro.

THE SLAVES OF LOMOORO, BY CHARLES NUETZEL

CHAPTER ELEVEN

Escape

As Jon heard the clicking of metal on stone, the footsteps of approaching men, he immediately considered the possibility of using the explosive pellets as a means of selling his life at a high price. Then he rejected it. At that moment he felt total defeat. But a shout sounded from the men ahead, and something hardened within him.

Suddenly Jon realized what he must attempt. If he could get on the other side of the warriors before they knew the Lients were in the corridor with them, he might have a chance. At least it was better than giving up all hope.

Then he saw the warriors start running toward him. They were holding swords, ready for combat. The corridor was six feet wide; the men were charging two abreast. They had little chance of using their weapons to any real advantage without endangering their companions. But if he were to get one of their swords, this would work to his advantage. They would get in each other's way if they did not re-group, while he could hack even awkwardly at them and still score mortal points.

Jon stood there, waiting, realizing that his best defense against the six armed warriors would be a well-timed and totally unexpected attack; this was something none of them would expect from an unarmed man.

He shifted the weight of his body. To all outward appearances he stood there as if defeated, hands at his sides, head drooped. But he had tensed every muscle, ready for instant play the moment the others were close enough to attack.

The men rushed up; it was apparent from their manner that they planned on surrounding him without any struggle. There was a casualness to their stride. Their sword points lowered—ever so slightly, but enough.

Jon waited until they were only a few feet away, edging along the walls of the corridor, taking up formation for flanking him. Then, without any warning, his body went into action—a well-trained machine of death. He did not put much conscious thought to what his hands were doing, merely letting all the years of training take over nerves and muscle. His right arm shot out, slashing into the neck of one warrior. His left hand stabbed at another with the arrow point aimed at the face like some small steel knife.

Neither man was killed, but the effect of his unexpected attack momentarily confused them. His third and fourth blows were aimed at the second pair of men in line. The one on his left doubled up as his fist sank into the man's stomach. He wrapped his right arm around the fourth warrior's neck, throwing him bodily against the last two warriors.

As the six men were attempting to adjust to a condition of battle, Jon grabbed the sword from the man he was holding. He leaped away, having now effectively managed to get to the far side of the Nal-Iean warriors.

He turned and faced his opponents; they could not come at him more than one at a time with any effect.

"Cut him down!" a voice shouted hysterically.

Jon tried to remember what he had learned about fencing, but knew it was far too little. All he could really hope for was to survive until the Lients came upon them.

The nearest man took a wild slice at Jon's head; it would have cut his skull in two if it had connected. He met the blow with the edge of his long sword. The clang of clashing metal reverberated from wall to wall along the corridor. A second man attempted to get at Jon with a thrust to his stomach, but he was easily pushed aside with the tip of his sword. Again the first man struck out, and Jon caught the sword once more with his own blade. Then, forgetting everything he had learned about swordplay, Jon grabbed his weapon with both hands and used it like an axe, slashing it from side to side, back and forth, up and down.

The others fell back in amazement at his unorthodox attack.

"Cut him down!" ordered their leader, who was now in the rear rank.

Immediately the front warrior lunged; Jon sidestepped, barely escaping the gleaming needle point. His own sword came down upon the man's skull, cutting a deep, bloody slash into flesh and bone. As the other fell to the floor, two more warriors took his place and Jon found himself facing two flashing swords.

A sense of defeat pressed Jon; he knew far better than the men now facing him just how short his training period had been. Then in a flash, as the two attacked at once, Jon realized that he did not have to follow instructions as given in that one-day lesson at the House of Balt-Lot. There were many ways to combat an enemy. Space Service training had prepared him for hand-to-hand combat against almost any weapon.

Desperation inspired his next move, for he saw two flashing points darting at his body.

Jon lunged, but instead of plunging with the point of his sword, he swung it downward in an arc for the first man's head and kicked with his right foot into the other man's body. The first received a cut in his head as the other doubled up in agony. A broad stroke with the blade stopped the next two men from rushing in for the kill. Then Jon leaped backwards, plunging his sword into the warrior who had received the crippling kick.

But now the other four rushed to attack, their swords flicking dangerously close. Jon felt the sting of two cuts drawn across his bare chest. His own sword stopped a downward slice from one warrior. He sidestepped a lunge which would have pinned him against the wall. He kicked out with his right foot, connecting against the side of one Nal-Iean swordsman and knocking the man off balance.

Jon spun away from the sting of a sword against his right arm. Just then he heard the low rumbling, a hideous growl from behind the warriors of Nal-Iò. Hope leaped into his heart; until that very moment, death had seemed only a sword-thrust away.

The four warriors turned, screaming as they saw the huge Lients crouching but a few yards away.

Jon didn't wait for a second look. He turned and raced down the corridor until he was some fifteen feet from the frightened warriors of Nal-Iò and the snarling Lients. Then he stopped. His first impulse was to throw one of the explosive pellets at them, more as an act of mercy than anything else. But the pellets were too scarce.

As he turned and started once more down the dimly lit corridor, Jon heard the snapping of jaws, the crunching of skulls, the screams of terror from men's throats. Jon had but one desire at that moment: to put as much distance as possible between himself and the feasting Lients.

He clutched the sword and felt a strange sense of power. He hadn't done too badly so far.

Unexpectedly, the corridor forked into two passages. Jon hesitated. These corridors might snake their way beneath the whole city of Nal-Iò, or they might circle back into the Arena itself. For a few moments he studied the two corridors, trying to decide which to take. Then he heard voices from the left one.

Quickly he stepped back into the right corridor and gripped his sword. Already a vague plan was forming in his mind. He needed an Arena warrior-guard's uniform. Dressed thus, he would easily be able to pass as a soldier of Nal-Iò.

The footsteps and voices came closer and closer. Then, as two men stepped into view and started down the corridor along which Jon had just come, he leaped from his hiding place and knocked one of the men down with the hilt of his sword.

The second Lomoorian turned and reached for the weapon strapped at his side. Jon didn't give the man time to draw the weapon. He lunged, smashing his left fist to the point of the other's jaw, knocking him backwards and to the floor against the wall.

Quickly Jon dragged the two men into the dark corridor and began to strip one of them of his harness.

Some minutes later, Jon stepped into the corridor and made his way in the direction from which the two now unconscious warriors had come. Dressed in the trappings of a warrior of Nal-Iò, Jon looked the same as any other guardsman. Harness leather crisscrossed over his chest and back, supporting the belt, long sword and knife—all cut and tooled in a beautifully detailed design.

His breath sucked in when he came to a cross corridor. Several warriors were making their way along the passage. Jon was alert to any signs of danger, but they paid little attention to him. Jon turned and followed a pair of men who were going toward what he hoped was the outside of the Arena.

Jon considered. He must find Red and Tanín. They could be anywhere along these corridors. There were cell doors every few yards now, and the sound of restless prisoners moving behind them. When he came to a side corridor which was darker than the rest, Jon turned and continued along this until he reached another turn, beyond which was almost total darkness. Slipping against the wall, he stood in the semi-gloom and tried to plan.

His temporary freedom could be snatched away at a moment's notice. Yet he was free for the first time in weeks—since being captured by the Rals.

Slowly a plan began to solidify in his mind. If it succeeded, he and all his friends would escape from the city of Nal-Iò. After that: Tal-Jaÿ.

How long he stood there listening and thinking in the semi-darkness, Jon had no way of judging. But slowly he became aware that there was less and less activity and noise, as if the Arena were settling down for the night. For some time after this he waited, listening, concentrating on his plan of action. Without Tanín their freedom was of doubtful value.

Jon crept out into the brighter corridor and carefully looked in both directions. No one was in sight. He tried to get his bearings, to decide which way would lead toward the outer wall, but he gave up. There was no way of knowing. Only then did he move along the corridor, taking a right turn.

He started humming softly. There were half a dozen

133

very popular tunes running their course of popularity throughout the Galactic Federation. One which was catchy and had been popular for some years was "Sing Me into Orbit!" He began to sing it now, raising the volume until it was loud enough to carry beyond the bolted doors of the cells lining the walls on either side. If Red were within hearing distance, Jon's plan would work. Red would know the song and recognize the language. To add to his chances of finding them, Jon added some names of his own: Red and Tanín. The first four lines, which were also the last four, ran:

> Sing me into Orbit
> Swing me to the skies
> Fly me to Dasorit
> But sing me no lies.

The song made no sense at all, and was not supposed to—a mere novelty number with a quick, sharp rhythm and beat which appealed to the teenagers. Jon added Red's name to the first and third lines, and Tanín's name to the second and fourth.

He moved casually along the corridor, but every muscle was alert for any sign of danger or discovery. His voice carried the tune in a raspy, off-beat manner, but the words rang out clearly:

> Sing me into Orbit, Red,
> Swing me to the skies, Tanín!
> Fly me to Dasorit, Red,
> But sing me no lies, Tanín!

Jon had gone some twenty feet along the corridor when a warrior entered the passageway from a cross corridor and headed his way.

As the man approached, Jon tensed, his right hand ready to reach for the sword. But to his relief the other passed by with only a nod.

Jon walked on, singing the song which he hoped Red or Tanín might hear. It was a crude way to call them out, but hopefully nobody else would notice. Even the man who had passed him had paid no attention, though by that time Jon had reverted to mumbling and humming over the words.

He moved along the passage to a crossing, then turned and went in the direction from which the warrior had come. Several times he passed other warriors, but they merely nodded. When he came to another corridor which crossed his, Jon hesitated, then saw the guard who stood there in the hallway. Immediately he recognized the man as the same one who had been on watch the night Londì had taken him to see Red.

Jon moved along the passageway and stepped directly up to the warrior-guard.

"Hello," he greeted, smiling. The man looked at Jon, recognition dawning in his face. Jon struck, fast—one at the pit of the stomach, a second blow to the side of the neck, then a third one on the back of the head as his knee slammed up to meet the man's face.

The fellow sank to the ground without a sound. No sooner had he struck the floor than Jon moved to a familiar-looking cell door. "Red! Tanín!"

He didn't wait for an answer before slipping the bolt from the wall and starting to open the door. He pulled the dead body of the guard up against the wall next to him.

Jon looked into the dim room and called out Red's name once more. All he could think of was the possibility that both of his friends might be dead. Yet they were his only hope. He held his breathe, listening. All he heard was the sound of hard breathing and occasional snores.

"Tanín! Red!" he called, louder now. The prisoners, quickly alert, came to their feet and swarmed in front of him.

Then he heard a voice call: "Jon!"

He recognized the voice and let out a sigh of relief. Then Red was standing in front of him, that mop of red-brown hair grown amazingly long and shaggy. The man looked like a true savage Lomoorian warrior-slave, standing there naked to the waist, hard muscles rippling smoothly at his shoulders and chest as he stepped forward and gripped Jon's right hand. Tanín was right behind him.

"How the hell did you get here?" Red demanded, his eyes darting behind Jon as if expecting to see officers.

"It's a long story, and there's no time!"

"Rockets, but it's good to see you!" Red grinned. "After the other night I got to thinkin' and started talkin' up a solar storm with Tanín. Once he was aimed at the right direction, he went right to destination and into orbit around the men, convincin' them it was a better idea to escape than stay warrior-slaves for their rocket-blastin' Games!"

Jon nodded. "We have to get out of here! Fast. Then get Mari!"

"It's insane!" Tanín told Jon. "We don't have a chance. But..."

Red laughed. "Better than dying here with no chance at all." Then he asked Jon, "Where do we go from here? How do we get out of the city?"

"One thing at a time. Fight our way out of the city, if necessary. I got out of the Arena by using the explosives. Have about fifteen or so left. Once outside the Arena, we can get Mari, *then* get out of Nal-Iò. First we want to get some weapons, though." He thought for a moment "if anybody here knows where the guards keep their weapons, we can arm ourselves and change into warrior harness. Then it will be easy to pass out of the city. If necessary, we fight our way out!"

A man's voice called out from he back of the cell. "I know where they are kept. Not far from here. It's a good plan!"

Tanín nodded as there were sounds of assent from those around them "What about the guard?" He indicated the man lying at Jon's feet

"Dead. Might get his uniform. Between the too of us it will be easy to march these 'prisoners' out into the corridor as if they're being escorted someplace else," Jon suggested.

Tanín shrugged. "It's as good a plan as any. In any case, it doesn't really matter. All these are well-trained fighting men. We all have death hanging over our heads, so that makes us even more desperate in combat. And we might not ever have another chance." He grinned at Jon. "You created quite a stir. After you left the Arena, the High Captain went into a rage. In order to punish whoever was responsible, he saw to it that the Games ended right there. That saved us this time. There might not be another chance of escaping. I'm with you, Jön-handön."

Jon's eyes quickly surveyed the dozen or so men surrounding him, Each was strongly built, obviously picked for strength and ability to handle weapons.

Jon motioned toward the dead man on the floor and without a word Tanín helped him drag the guard into the cell. They closed the door and then stripped the man. A few minutes later, Tanín was dressed in the uniform of the Nal-Iò warrior guard, armed with sword and knife. The expression on his features was one of pure joy—but a grim kind of joy. Quite obviously Tanín felt half a man without weapons. Possession of sword and knife and a warrior's uniform had transformed him into a killing animal, dangerous to all enemies.

"Well," Tanín said brusquely, "let's get out of here!"

Jon opened the door and led the way into the corridor.

They filed out one at a time, Jon in front and Tanín taking a position behind, so that if they came across any Nal-Iian warriors it might appear that the others were still under guard. But this precaution proved unnecessary. The man who had claimed to know the way to the guard room walked behind Jon, giving verbal directions. They had to go only a few hundred feet from the cell, make turns down a couple of other corridors, and suddenly found themselves in a small hallway which ended at an open door. But standing in front of the door was a warrior. He turned and stared at them.

Before the man could question them, Jon had knocked him unconscious, dragged his body into the room beyond, and motioned the others to follow. The walls of the room were lined with uniforms and weapons, and his fellow prisoners quickly made their way toward the racks upon which they hung.

After the last man had filed into the room, Jon closed the door, then urged all of them to hurry.

Red moved close as Jon quickly told them about his escape from the Arena. When finished, he added: "Now what we have to do is get Mari. There isn't any time to waste!"

"Think she's okay?" Red asked.

"As far as I know. Unless they decided I was dead! If so,

Balt-Lot will be all too anxious to take her to bed! He has been waiting for my death," Jon hissed, anxious to get started. "We have to get out of here. If anybody knows the way, speak up!"

He surveyed the group. The man who had led them to the weapons room nodded. "There is a shorter way..."

Once again they went in single file, all silent and grim, into the corridor, this time behind the man who could guide them out of the Arena building. They seemed to twist aimlessly for some time, and Jon could not help fearing that somehow they might be led into a trap. But before long they came to a stairway and moved silently up it. By the time they reached the top, Jon was breathing a sigh of relief. This was the same staircase down which Londì had taken him the evening he had come to see Red.

As they stepped into the archway which led from the Arena to the streets of Nal-Iò, the night air chilled through Jon's body. It was the coldest night he had experienced on Lomooro, which was normally quite hot and tropical even at night.

Red and Tanín conferred with Jon before they stepped out into the city night.

"Where to from here?" Red asked.

Before answering, Jon said: "What about these men?"

"They will follow us," Red assured him. Then he frowned uncertainly at Tanín. "Right?"

"As far as the jungle. Then, once our mutual interests are served, they will scatter. I think the whole idea is fantastic. It's never been done before—or at least not successfully for so long a time that nobody ever even considers escaping once they are captured." Then Tanín grinned. "But I must admit once you put the thought in my mind, it wasn't hard for Red here to convince me. The idea is appealing."

"Come, this is not the time for light conversation. This way." Jon started toward the open gate.

Once outside in the city proper, the three took immediate command of the small band, Jon being the natural leader.

"We have a woman to pick up first—then we leave Nal-

Iò" Jon's announcement was a command. "It will take but a short while, and possibly there will be mounts at the same place. I have magic which we can fall back on, if necessary. Are you with me?"

The others murmured their agreement without hesitation.

"Fine. As long as we stay together, we will be strong enough to fight our way out of the city without any trouble."

The others nodded, but this time said nothing. When Jon turned and started to lead the way down the street, he felt a strong sense of power, but at the same time a nervous awareness of unrest. Numbers might be to their advantage in a fight, but could easily work against them when trying to move silently and unnoticed through the streets. In the moments that followed, his fears proved groundless. The rattle of swords in sheaths was kept to a minimum.

The night was dark and the buildings loomed overhead like shadowy figures; the wind slipped through the streets with a ghostly whisper.

Jon was vaguely aware of the change which had come over him in the time he had been on Lomooro. His life had been devoted to becoming a soldier for the greater glory of the Federation and the honor of the name of Handon. Yet the great glory of the Federation meant little now, and the honor of Handon had become simply the survival of Handon. Fighting for the sake of glory now seemed unimportant— there were more urgent goals. Escape. Survival, freedom and life.

And Mari.

They moved along the streets for some time before Jon suddenly spied a familiar building. It was the House of Balt-Lot.

Jon held up his hand. "I'm going in. Wait for me. If I don't return shortly, go in after me!" He turned to Red. "About twenty minutes at most. Get Mari, by force if necessary. Find my body and take the explosives!"

Jon strode across the street and through the side entrance. As he passed Londì's door, he fought down the temptation to wake the man. Later, if it was possible. Mari was most important.

Jon slipped into the hall which Londì had told him led to the female quarters. Darkness was deep on all sides; for a moment he felt lost. Then a scream sounded from the far side of the house. There was no mistaking the voice. Then he heard, in the Galactic language, the word: "Help!"

Jon whirled and ran toward the voice. Long training had taught him how to move silently.

As he came into the main corridor of the house, Jon hesitated for a moment, listening. Strangely enough, no doors opened, no warrior-slaves appeared, no female voices giggled or stirred. Possibly it was typical of a new female slave to resist the lust-crazed master of the house on her first night in his bed chambers. Apparently orders had been given to ignore such screams. Maybe nobody slept in this wing. Nonetheless, nobody responded to Mari's scream.

Jon froze, listening. Then he heard the sound of pottery smashing against a wall, and a slow smile formed on his lips. He turned toward the sound. Another scream slashed the night air like the sharp edge of a sword cutting through human flesh. Jon came to a stop in front of a closed door.

"Mari!" he shouted.

A curse and scream answered him, followed by the voice of Lord Balt-Lot. "Go away, you fool!"

Jon pressed against the door, then stepped back and slammed forcefully against it with all the weight of his body. Again he backed to the far wall of the hall, and this time hit the wooden structure with his foot, splintering the door away from its metal latch. Sword in hand, he rushed into the room, slamming the door shut behind him.

The man turned, a hissing sound trembling from his thick lips. Eyes bulged as he saw Jon. He had been in the process of forcing Mari down upon a huge bed. Her filmy gown had been ripped in several places. The room was bare except for two small stands on each side of the bed. On one of them lay a large, purple vase.

Lord Balt-Lot lunged for the harness lying at the foot of the bed. A moment later he swung a gleaming jewel-encrusted sword through the air as he came savagely at Jon. The man moved so quickly that it was almost impossible to prepare a defense. For a heavy man, Lord Balt-Lot was

140

amazingly agile.

Jon caught the other's sword with the edge of his own and then moved quickly, hoping to end the fight before it had really begun. He had no plans to cross swords with Lord Balt-Lot, who was surely far more skilled in using the weapon.

But the other man leaped back; the point of his sword flicked Jon's chest, drawing blood. Then Lord Balt-Lot attacked, pushing forward like a mad man, his sword moving like lightning, lunging, cutting, hacking. Half a dozen times in the first minute, he cut bloody scratches along Jon's half-naked body. The man's thick lips spread in a wide grin of pleasure. In a matter of moments, Jon would be run through.

"Enjoying yourself, *slave?*" taunted Lord Balt-Lot, bringing the point of his sword forward and drawing it across Jon's stomach to paint a thin line of red. "I could have cut your guts with that, but all in good time. You will soon learn the art of sword play as no instructor might teach it. Of course, it will do you no good!"

Again the point leaped out, this time touching Jon's right side. "You see, once a man knows his weapon, it is easy to control it. As a great cook will know how to season a dish, so a Master will know how to just barely draw blood, or..." The man lunged, but this time Jon leaped back, avoiding death by an inch.

Lord Balt-Lot grinned. "Nothing like a good duel before feasting on the rewards."

He laughed and then came at Jon more slowly, his face suddenly deadly and hard. "But the games are over, my foolish friend!"

CHAPTER TWELVE

Two Lomoorian Lovers

During the first minutes of the fight, Mari had remained paralyzed on the bed watching the deadly battle. Jon had seen her in quick, flashing moments, and each time felt that this might be his last image of her before he died. Then out of the corner of his eye he saw Mari burst into action, leaping for the table at her left and grabbing the large vase. At that moment Lord Balt-Lot came in close, his face tensed for the kill. Jon used every ounce of strength and skill to put the man off for only a moment longer, to give Mari the chance to follow through with her planned move—one which might save his life.

The gleaming blade sliced at Jon as he sidestepped in a desperate attempt to escape death.

Then Mari rushed in from behind Lord Balt-Lot, vase raised high over her head. The man lunged, point extended. Jon felt the cold steel press against his stomach. Then the vase smashed down on the man's skull.

With one motion Jon knocked the sword away from his body, then gasped in relief as Lord Balt-Lot slumped slowly to the floor, a surprised expression frozen on his thick features.

For only a moment Jon stood looking from the unconscious man to Mari and back again. A slow grin spread across his face. "Thanks."

"I…I thought you were dead!" Mari whispered, coming slowly closer. For a moment she stood in front of him, looking up into his eyes. Then suddenly she was in his arms, trembling, her lips close. "Oh, thank God you're alive. They said you were dead..."

Jon comforted Mari. As he held her near, he felt a strange surge of emotion which he had never experienced before. It was a mixture of physical excitement and desire, and something else which at first was hard to place or label. All his life women had been something to merely desire physically, but this was a new feeling. Up until then Jon had not known how he felt toward Mari, thinking it was only the urge to protect her because she was in a way his responsibility. Now he began to realize the true feeling he had for her.

He said: "We have to get out of here." His voice was husky with emotion. "There's no time."

"But where?" she asked in a frightened voice, looking at him.

"Tanín and Red are outside with several other men. What we need are mounts. Then we'll leave this place and go to Tanín's home city, where there will be friends."

She merely nodded; as he moved toward the door, she followed without a word. As they went into the hallway, Jon moved to the room where Londì had been. Once opposite the door, Mari asked nervously, "What are you doing?"

"Londì. Maybe he will go with us. We talked about it. And we could use such a man as Londì." Then Jon opened the door, drew the knife from his harness and approached the sleeping man. He was upon the other before Mari had even entered the room.

Jon's knife went to Londì's throat as he shook the man gently awake. If the Lomoorian tried to call out an alarm, there would be little choice but to silence him.

The Champion of the House of Balt-Lot awakened. He stiffened as he looked up at the form above him.

Jon grinned. "You said you might go with me if I could prove a great warrior with great magic."

Londì jerked with shock; his jaw moved against the pressure of the knife. "What are you doing here?"

"You coming with me?" Jon asked. "I couldn't leave without giving you a chance. Freedom—complete—or your life as it has been here."

Londì nodded slowly as the knife moved from his throat.

Jon put the knife back in its sheath. "Come. We have to leave immediately. We need mounts, about fifteen. Does Balt-Lot have them?"

"Yes, beyond the slave quarters." Londì reached for his harness. "Why so many mounts?"

"We took along some fellow prisoners. Now hurry. There's little time. Balt-Lot is unconscious."

"Did you have a chance to kill him?"

Jon shrugged.

"If you had a chance, you should have killed him," Londì said.

"Hurry!" Jon realized that it would have been better to kill Balt-Lot. Yet he had not been able to kill an unconscious man.

Silently the three slipped from the room and moved down the hall. With Londì at the lead, they went through a side door which led back of the slaves' quarters. Jon could immediately hear the sounds of restless animals moving in a fenced area.

"Here," Londì announced, pointing. "And we can leave through the back. Where are your men?"

"In front of the house, across the street," came Jon's reply. He was already trying to figure out their best chance of escaping the city.

"You are a mad fellow," Londì grinned as they moved toward the animal stockade, "but a brave and daring one. And what magic your escape from the Arena was! Great magic!"

Without any further conversation, the two men entered the animal compound and gathered the eight mounts which were there.

"We need more," Jon told the other man.

"We'll have to ride double."

As they led the animals out through the back gate, Jon heard noise from the house. He whispered, "Hurry."

Mari was moving close to him, as if attempting to find comfort and protection in his nearness. When they went into the street, Jon remembered the atomatic explosive pellets which had been hidden under his mattress. He whispered to Londì:

"Did they touch my bed since I left?"

The other nodded. "When they changed it, they found some strange stones. Balt-Lot gave them to the High Captain as a curiosity, in an attempt to win favor."

Jon nodded grimly. Nothing could be done about the loss. The pellets which were left could be used only in an emergency.

At that moment Jon suddenly became aware of the fact that he accepted their isolation on this planet as a possibly lifetime affair. Chances seemed slight that he could get to one of the other scout-boats which might have landed on Lomooro and find a radio beam working. He found the fact surprisingly easy to accept. If fact, quite desirable. Here on Lomooro it might be a far better life, simple, near Nature, with these new friends.

As they made their way across the street toward the shadows in which his companions were still waiting, Jon heard shouts from the House of Balt-Lot. Balt-Lot had regained consciousness and was screaming for help. It was only a matter of minutes before pursuit would follow.

Jon called, "Red, Tanín, hurry, all of you! We have to double up on these beasts. Mount and head for the city gate!"

Jon watched Londì, who grabbed hold of the animal's ears as a means of pulling himself onto the animal. Jon followed suit. There was neither harness nor saddle on the beasts.

"How do you guide them?" Red asked Tanín.

"Grab the ears and pull them, the left one for left, the right one for right. Kick its sides if you want to go forward, pull gently on the ears if you want to stop," Tanín explained, helping Red up behind him. "You don't have to worry about that, anyway. Just hold on tight!"

The others laughed at the last remark. Jon pulled Mari up behind him just as a heavy figure came running out of the House of Balt-Lot, waving a sword in his right hand.

Londì, who had just mounted his Martos, jerked the right ear of the animal. He drew his sword and went charging down upon his former master, the weapon flashing in the dim light.

The clang of steel hitting steel rang out through the night. All the former slave-prisoners turned and stared at this unexpected battle.

Lord Balt-Lot was amazingly good, making an excellent show of himself against the mounted Champion, but the battle could not last long, for the Champion of the House of Balt-Lot was far better at killing than the Master. Then, just as Londì's blade sank into Lord Balt-Lot's chest, a flock of warriors came running out of the house behind the two combatants. When they saw their Master fall, they started for his killer.

A string of vile words burst from Red as he leaped from his mount. With drawn sword he met one of the warriors. Tanín was quickly at his side.

For a moment Jon had a chance to see an amazing display of swordsmanship from Red, considering that the man had only learned how to handle the weapon during his stay in Nal-Iò. But expert as it seemed, Red was no match for his opponent. In that flashing moment, Jon realized that their escape was for nothing if he did not rally the men in one united effort, and fast, before they were cut down or finally outnumbered. Everyone outside of himself had by now entered the battle in the street. Jon had hesitated because of Mari mounted behind him. Already the sound of combat was attracting the attention of people in surrounding houses.

"Hold on!" he shouted to Mari as he grabbed the ears of his mount and pressed his heels against the animal's side. To Jon's amazement, the beast understood what he wanted. Before Jon had time to even get sword in hand, the Martos had skillfully moved into position for the kill, just behind Red's attacker.

Jon raised the sword high over his head and was about to swing it downward, when he got a good look at the man fighting Red.

"Fal!" Jon shouted. "Stop, Red! Fal, stop!"

Immediately the two men froze, their swords poised in mid-air. One moment more and Red would have been dead—the point of Fal's weapon was only inches from his chest.

"Fal, join us. Come with us!" Jon quickly offered. He had barely finished his statement when Fal whipped around and dipped the point of his sword into one of the Balt-Lot warriors who had just rushed up.

"Let's get out of here!" Jon yelled at the top of his voice, waving his sword high over his head in an attempt to attract the attention of his men. As he did so, he surveyed the street into which had crowded some twenty men from the House of Balt-Lot. A couple of his men already lay dead on the ground. They were already hopelessly outnumbered, and even as his words were spoken, he realized that defeat would come within seconds unless something was done at once.

Urging his mount toward the outer fringes of the fighting men, Jon reached into one of his pocket pouches and pulled out an explosive pellet. With the tip of his bloody sword he nicked the pellet, waited a couple of seconds, and then threw the explosive just behind the nearest Balt-Lot warriors.

The blast which followed seemed like a bomb in the close confines of the street. Already doors and windows were opening and people peered out to see what was happening.

"Let's get out of here!" Jon shouted, already moving toward one of the two men fighting Tanín. He cut the fellow down before the man knew what hit him. Tanín ran the other man through.

"Hurry!" Jon cried.

Immediately his men began to fight their way through the stunned warriors of the House of Balt-Lot, who were not only overwhelmed by the slaves' revolt, but especially shocked by the explosion which they surely would consider powerful magic.

Fal found one of the mounts and leaped upon its back. Jon, with Mari behind him, urged his mount at full speed down the street, not even bothering to look back.

They headed straight for the city gate. Jon shouted the group to a halt. Already the windows around them were opening and curious heads peeped out.

"We have to fight our way out of the city," Jon announced. 'We'll crash our way through the gate if

148

necessary. Okay?"

The others nodded.

"Slaves! They are escaped slaves!" a distant voice bellowed from the direction of the House of Balt-Lot.

Jon cried: "Run for it now! Head for the gate!"

In a mass they urged their mounts down the street. Behind them came the sound of pursuit.

The charge to the gate seemed to take an endless time. Jon heard voices from behind, screaming for them to stop. The warriors at the gate turned and drew their swords, ready to meet the charge. Upon the city wall, warriors turned and fitted arrows to their bows.

What happened after that was blurred, for they charged down upon the gate guards like savage beasts, attacking without mercy. Then the din of battle surrounded them on all sides. They cut down the four gate guards in the first few seconds of battle. Tanín dismounted and worked the gate controls as arrows shot through the air from the wall above, some hitting mounts and men, others sinking harmlessly into the ground. Then the Nal-Iean warriors who were pursuing them suddenly attacked from behind.

Jon turned his mount and slashed through the air with his sword, cutting into the head of one Lomoorian. He felt the pressure of Mari's arms tighten around his waist. "Through the gate, fast!" he roared.

The battle was all but over now. Several men fought it out to the end on the fringes, but in a matter of minutes it would all be over. As the gate slowly swung open, the last of the guards fell dead.

All that was left of his small band was seven men.

They were standing scattered, swords dangling in their hands.

"Okay, let's leave." As Jon spoke, a cry of pain sounded from behind him. He turned to see Fal crumple to the ground with an arrow deep in his chest.

Like birds scattering, the others moved for their mounts. Jon kicked his Martos toward the gate. An arrow flew past his head, sinking into the ground as the mount moved forward. One man fell from his mount with a thin feathered shaft piercing his body. Jon could hear arrows twanging through the air all around him. It seemed as if all the warriors of Nal-Iò were firing at them as they streaked beyond the city gates.

The jungle was some two thousand yards from the walls of Nal-Iò, across the neatly trimmed farm land. They closed the distance much faster than he might have thought, for the Martos shot across the fields like speeding ground cars.

During the flight to the edge of the jungle, Jon once again felt the sense of strangeness which had touched him several times in the past. Here he was, a Galactic Spaceman, riding a strange animal across a grassy Lomoorian plain, all but naked, sword strapped to his side, and outwardly no different in appearance than the people of the planet. He felt a deep awareness of the change which had taken place since crash-landing on the planet. Professional Galactic soldier, or warrior of Lomooro, it made little difference. On Lomooro you killed one man at a time. In the Galactic war, it was possible to exterminate the inhabitants of an entire solar system with the pressing of a button, and seldom did one kill less than half a dozen men at the same time on ground attack. The difference was a matter of degree.

They were already entering the outer fringes of the jungle as Jon's mind returned to the immediate present. Once the trees had thickened, gathering together in a tangle of vines and brush, Jon pulled his mount to a halt, calling to the others to do the same.

Londì looked worriedly toward the city of Nal-Iò, all but hidden by the surrounding forest and early morning darkness. "They will be coming after us soon."

Tanín countered thoughtfully. "Not necessarily. They might decide to leave us to the Lients and other jungle animals!"

Jon turned to Tanín. "Where to now? Which direction?"

"Toward the rising sun to the River Boltor, then left, down river to the coast and to Tal-Jaÿ!" Tanín explained.

Londì frowned. "Why Tal-Jaÿ?"

"I am Warrior Lord and will see to it that you are all received as friends."

Londì was not so easily convinced. "How do I know you are telling the truth?"

"You will be no worse off than before—and better off than in the jungle," Tanín countered, smiling, his eyes sparkling in the semi-darkness.

Londì reluctantly nodded. "Tal-Jaÿ it is."

Jon grinned, examined the remaining members of his band, and thought what a savage little group they were. Almost everybody was covered with blood, but there was a brightness in their eyes that he had not noticed before in the eyes of any Lomoorians. Only Tanín, Londì, Red, Mari and himself had survived. He regretted deeply the loss of Fal; he had liked the young warrior. But nothing could be done about it now.

As they started in the direction Tanín had said would take them around the city of Nal-Iò and finally along the cliffs, Mari looked up at Jon. She turned her head and asked, "Where to now? I mean, once we get to this city of Tanín's? What happens to us then?"

"We have to make the best of what life gives us." He had to force the next words out of his mouth. "It's best that we all accept our life here."

"But..." Her eyes moistened. For a moment it looked as if Mari was about to lose control, then her lips compressed. "Then there's no hope of returning home—leaving this planet?"

"There's always hope, and I won't give it up. But... it is better if we accept things as they are, and make the best of it. Hope, yes. No more than hope, though."

He felt the drag of depression at having to tell Mari this cold, harsh truth. But the fact remained that their chances of returning to the society and civilization which had given them birth was slight, and he did not want to give her false hopes.

The night began to dull. The sun slowly crept over the horizon. Tanín finally brought his mount to a halt. "I think the cliffs shouldn't be far from here. We should go on more carefully now. Keep a look out for any break in the underbrush."

They had been traveling for some time in a wide circle through the jungles surrounding Nal-Iò. So far no sign of pursuit had presented itself.

151

Mari had fallen asleep on Jon's arms; her head rested lightly on his chest. It was pleasant holding her. He was painfully aware of the softness of her body where it touched his, and the urge to hold her closer, to kiss those full red lips, was at times all but impossible to ignore.

"Well have to find a path down the cliffs," Londì pointed out. "And from what I understand, that might be difficult. The one path which the people of Nal-Iò use in the only good way down. We might have to leave our mounts behind."

Tanín nodded. "Maybe it might be just as safe on foot. We might as well take a look about. I heard there were a few crude footpaths leading down the cliff."

They continued for a short distance, and as Tanín had suggested, the cliffs were quite close. All at once the jungle thinned and abruptly they were standing at the edge of the cliffs, overlooking the jungle below.

The thick tropical forest spread out before them in a seemingly endless tide of tangled purplish vegetation. There was no immediate path down the cliff, though.

Tanín suddenly pointed. "Look! Water! The River Boltor cuts close here."

Jon looked and saw the glittering sparkle which might have been water. Then as he followed along toward their right, he saw what looked like a wide cutting nearer to the cliffs.

Tanín chuckled. "If we find a way down where the river is close to the cliffs, it will be easy from then on. We can camp on the bank of the river tonight and start building a raft tomorrow. In a couple of days we will be in Tal-Jaÿ."

Jon nodded. "We might as well follow the cliffs until we find a way down."

Londì looked grim. "But we have to go in that direction." He pointed to their right. "And it takes us near the Caverns of Death."

Tanín shrugged, unconcerned. "It can't be far to some means of getting down the cliffs. We'll have little trouble."

They continued along the narrow edge of the cliff which was for the most part clear of jungle growth, being covered by a blue-tinted grass. The sun was quite high in the heavens by the time Tanín shouted, "Looks like a way down. The cliff is broken here!" He was looking over the cliff. As he dismounted, he motioned the others to his side.

They urged their mounts forward. Jon helped Mari dismount and slid down beside her. They stepped to the edge of the cliff. For a moment everyone was silent, looking across the misty expanse of the jungle and down along the steep cliff.

Red cursed. "We can't take the mounts with us down that."

"But it is close to the river," Tanín pointed out.

Jon nodded. The narrow trail was nothing more than a foothold, but just beyond a short stretch of jungle was the river. His only concern was for Mari.

Would she be able to make it down the face of the cliff? For that matter, would any of them be able to climb down such a dangerous route?

"There's no better way?" He looked at Tanín.

The man shook his head. "We've been traveling all morning. The farther we go in this direction the worse it will be. Those cliffs, I have heard, go many days' march. Farther along these cliffs are the Caverns of the Dead—nobody has ever returned from there alive! Death waits, breathes hotter and hotter in this direction." Tanín nodded to their right. "And, anyway, if you look down a short distance there is a fairly comfortable-looking ledge along the cliff. Looks like an animal trail. I think we can lower ourselves one at a time from here to the ledge below. From then on it shouldn't be too difficult." Tanín was looking at Mari as he spoke. "There's no better way. This has every advantage we might wish for under the circumstances."

Londì put in, "Tanín is right, Jön-handön. The Caves of the Dead are not to be tempted."

"What are they?" Mari asked, wide-eyed.

"Caverns in the Great Mountain where the Fire God breathes and belches water of fiery rock in hot Waves of burning death. The Wot-tons live there, and they search far for slaves to work the Yellow Mines."

"Talking will get us nowhere!" Jon stated, now taking command of the group once more. "We had better get down to the river before darkness. I wouldn't want to be caught going down that pathway at night.

The others agreed. In a short time Londì was lowered to the ledge below, which was only a foot in width. One by one the others were lowered beside him, Jon insisting on being last, Mari going down just before him. Then slowly Jon let himself down over the face of the cliff and felt hands grab him a moment later. His feet seemed to dangle in space, then gratefully he felt his sandals touch solid ground. A moment later he was standing beside his friends.

The long descent to the ground below was an endless torture of suspense. One wrong move meant death. Once Mari slipped, but Jon caught her just in time.

Jon had to keep himself from looking down. He had made that mistake once, and for a moment dizziness had threatened almost overwhelmingly. Yet at the instant when he believed death might engulf him, his first thought was for Mari. His main concern now was for this woman whom he had discovered a great love when holding her close for the first time in the bed chambers of Lord Balt-Lot of Nal-Iò. The amazing thing was that he had found love under such adverse and strange circumstances. It was hardly the right time for romance.

All his life, the idea of falling in love with a woman had seemed childishly romantic. Men merely joined their lives with a Woman and had children by her—nothing more. Too many hard years had gone by, living in the Space Service, taking up with the space port girls who hung around the saloons to keep company with the Spacemen who visited their worlds. Love of the kind which could be enjoyed between man and woman for life was totally new to him. His own father and mother had merely been living companions who shared the same house and produced the same child. But there was no secret that his father has been in the company of many other women, like most of the other married Spacemen.

So, as they made their way down the cliffs of Nal-Iò, Jon's thoughts were touched by the memory of holding Mari close, and his newly discovered deep love for her. That she might return this love was something he could not even allow himself to consider.

The hot tropic sun was sinking toward the horizon by the time they came to the last few feet of the narrow pathway. It ended some ten feet from the ground below.

"I'll lower myself," Tanín said, since he was first in line. "Then we can go over one at a time."

He jumped off the ledge and landed as if springs were attached to his sandals. He rolled forward and then stood, turned and grinned.

Jon helped lower Mari to Tanín and afterward waited until the other two men had followed. Then Jon looked up, amazed at the height from which they had originally descended. The effort had been torturous. Every muscle ached. He could only imagine how Mari must feel. He jumped down beside the others.

"Let's camp here," Jon suggested, glancing at Mari. "We're in a clearing, and after gathering wood..."

"No Jon!" Tanín warned shaking his head. "We can make a River Boltor in less than an hour. Tomorrow we will build a large raft and let the river carry us to the city of Tal-Jaÿ."

Jon hesitated, then shrugged, realizing that Tanín was right. He had let his concern about Mari influence his judgment. He looked up at the darkened sky. Shortly it would be total night "What about the night beasts?"

"We can get up into the trees," Londì answered. "Cut some branches of fern, spread them over the interlocking branches, and have good, safe beds."

With that the group started toward the edge of the jungle, some twenty yards from the cliffs, and began cutting through the underbrush. The river had appeared to be only a short distance from the cliffs when looking down upon it, but now it seemed as if they were never going to make it before death stalked them down. The darkness pressed harder and closer around them. Then suddenly they came to a game trail and Tanín, who was in the lead, started off to the left. Shortly they came to the river which murmured loudly as it rolled along.

For a moment Jon stood looking at the greenish river which was some two hundred yards wide at this point. It was a refreshing sight.

Then Tanín said: "We had better fix the bedding."

Londì pointed out strong-stemmed fern which had lacy vegetation matted around it. It grew plentifully all around them. "These we cut, at the base. They are strong enough to support a man's weight. Lay them on some securely interlocking branches of the trees, at the height of two men. After you have a comfortable and firmly packed area to support your whole body, stretched out full length, you have a safe bed." As Londì spoke, he pointed out several yellowish fern which he considered best for their purposes. Tanín was already beginning to cut some of the fern leaves at the base of their branches where they grew outward from the plants.

Immediately everybody started picking the firm leaves. Mari helped by pointing to what looked like good branches for Jon to cut. In a very short time they had gathered more than enough for the five of them.

Tanín leaped into a nearby tree, pulled himself up branch by branch. Londì followed immediately. The two worked like a well-trained team, even though neither of them spoke.

"Hand up the branches," Londì instructed from his perch in the trees, several branches below Tanín.

Jon quickly did as instructed and the other two followed his example. It wasn't long before all the branches had been lifted up to Tanín, who spread them out, making a large pile of the fern high up in the trees.

"Okay," Londì said, "up you fellows come."

Some time later, after the sun had settled behind the horizon and total darkness had settled around them, Jon, who was lying only a few feet away from Mari and some distance from the others in their tree camp, said: "Not much like a real bed, is it?"

The tone of Mari's voice as she answered was startling. "Does it really make much difference?"

He might have expected bitterness in her voice, but she sounded like a woman who really meant what she said.

Jon sat up and stared at Mari. In the dim light he could make out the shape of her face, but not her expression. Yet somehow he could not help thinking she was smiling.

"Probably the beds will be better in Tal-Jaÿ," he offered.

"They *were* comfortable in Nal-Iò, but not quite as wonderful," she murmured. "Nor was the food of Nal-Iò, though hot, as good as the fruit that Tanín and Londì gathered."

"Wonderful?" Jon was puzzled by her statement.

"Well, you might say that working as a slave was not the most comfortable work for a woman like myself."

"A woman of culture and taste and quality?" Jon offered, feeling that sense of helplessness he experienced every time he thought of Mari and his new-found love.

"A woman—only," she replied. He saw her form slipping closer; an arm reached toward him. She took hold of his hand. "I'm only a woman, Jon," she whispered. "And as a woman on this savage Lomooro, I think we should adapt and quietly accept the reality around us."

The contact of her hand made it suddenly impossible for him to speak. He merely nodded.

"And," she continued gently, her voice filled with husky emotion, "I do think we have all changed. I realize now that there is an equality which goes beyond the class in which humans put themselves; the labels and names by which others call us. The quality of soul and heart."

She was silent for a long time. Jon searched for words, trying to believe what hers seemed to imply. Then suddenly his lips moved; words which were unexpectedly honest burst out.

"I love you, Mari. I'd die for you!" Immediately he was afraid he had gone too far.

She merely said, "I know, Jon." After a long silence, she continued. "Jon, I think this is our world. I don't think we will ever leave it. Do you?"

He realized she did not expect him to answer that question.

"Jon, the way I acted when the three of us were crowded into the space-boat—I don't think that should apply to you. Never you, again."

Even Jon was able to accept the total meaning of her words. Even Jon Handon, Spaceman, Lomoorian Warrior, savage, knew that Mari Dorna, daughter of wealth, culture and High Galactic Society, woman of Lomooro, savage, had made one of the most direct moves a woman could make to a man and still retain her dignity.

Without another word, Jon moved over to her. It was a distance of only a foot, but it had seemed more than a million miles until a few seconds before. She came eagerly into his arms and for a long moment they held one another close, their lips touching in a warm, sweet kiss. She trembled slightly as her hands gently pressed against his chest.

"I wonder how they do it here," she mused, looking up into his eyes.

"Probably the same way they do it all over the universe!" Jon laughed, throatily.

"Well, in time don't you think we'd better find out?" She pushed firmly until he was at arm's distance. "But even here on Lomooro I think a woman should do things in the right manner, don't you?"

Jon wanted to shout, to laugh, to dance. But instead he gently forced Mari's hands away and lifted her up into his arms. For a long time they kissed, then slowly he released her and moved away. A moment later he was lying on his own fern bedding.

A great surge of contentment waved through him as he lay there thinking about Mari and their future on Lomooro. He realized the only thing that really mattered was not where they were, but that they were together.

He finally whispered, "Mari, I think you're right. The moment we get to Tal-Jaÿ, we'll do whatever they do to join hearts and souls eternally together."

Her lilting laughter was soft. "Souls, maybe, but as for my heart, you could never have more of it than you already have."

"Goodnight, Mari," he said. He gripped her fingers with his own as she reached across the short gap between their fern beds high in the trees on the banks of the River Boltor on the planet Lomooro.

"Goodnight, Jon, my love."

As they fell asleep, their fingers still touching, they were, for the first time since landing on the planet, two

Lomoorians—two savage Lomoorian lovers willing to bravely face the future, no matter what it might bring, together.

About the Author

Charles Nuetzel was born in San Francisco in 1934, and writes:

"As long as I can remember I wanted to be a writer. It was a dream I never thought would materialize. But with the help of Forrest J Ackerman, who became my agent, I managed to finally make it into print.

"I was lucky enough not only in selling my work to publishers but also ending up packaging books for some of them, and finally becoming a 'publisher' much like those who had bought my first novels. From there it as a simple leap to editing not only a sci-fi anthology, but a line of sci-fi books for Powell Sci-Fi back in the 1960s. Throughout these active professional years I had the chance to design some covers and do graphic cover layouts for pocket books & magazines."

Much of his work in covers and graphics are a result of having had a father who was a professional commercial artist, and who did a number of covers for sci-fi magazines in the 1950s and later for pocket books—even for some of Mr. Nuetzel's books.

In retirement he has become involved in swing dancing, a long time lover of Big Band jazz. But more interestingly world travels have taken him (and his wife Brigitte) across the world, to Hawaii, Caribbean, Mexico, Kenya, Egypt, Peru, having a lifelong interest in ancient civilizations. His website is full of thousands of pictures taken during these trips.